MEDIEVAL MAYHEM

MIDDLE SCHOOL MAYHEM SERIES: BOOK FIVE

C.T. WALSH

FARCICAL PRESS

Publisher's Cataloging-in-Publication Data provided by Five Rainbows Cataloging Services

Names: Walsh, C.T., author.

Title: Medieval mayhem / C.T. Walsh.

Description: Bohemia, NY : Farcical Press, 2019. | Series: Middle school mayhem, bk. 5. | Summary: When Austin is publicly embarrassed by baby-faced villain Randy Warblemacher, he drops the gauntlet at the Medieval Renaissance Fair. | Audience: Grades 5 & up. | Also available in ebook and audiobook formats.

Identifiers: ISBN 978-1-950826-04-9 (paperback)

Subjects: LCSH: Bildungsromans. | CYAC: Middle school students--Fiction. | Middle schools--Fiction. | Renaissance fairs--Fiction. | Bullying--Fiction. | Humorous stories. | BISAC: JUVENILE FICTION / Social Themes / Adolescence & Coming of Age. | JUVENILE FICTION / School & Education. | JUVENILE FICTION / Humorous Stories. | JUVENILE FICTION / Boys & Men.

Classification: LCC PZ7.1.W35 Me 2019 (print) | LCC PZ7.1.W35 (ebook) | DDC [Fic]--dc23.

COVER CREDITS

Cover design by Books Covered
Cover photographs © Shutterstock
Cover illustrations by Maeve Norton

For my Family

Thank you for all of your support

1

Behold, noble subjects. It is I, Sir Austin Davenport the Hilarious. The tale I shall tell this day with my most mysterious of voices brings us back to medieval times. It is a tale of betrayal, courage in the face of impossible odds, blood-curdling hatred, enduring love, horrifying sights like my principal in tights, and triumph over evil and nightmares, mainly of my principal in tights.

The tale begins in the dark ages. No, not medieval times. Middle school. The first day of seventh grade, to be exact. We started right where we left off. War. No, I'm not being dramatic.

My best friend, Ben, and I walked in the creaky double doors and soaked in all the gloriousness of Cherry Avenue Middle School, which was basically just my girlfriend, Sophie, who I spotted across the atrium. A smile spread across my face as I walked toward her.

"This year is going to be so much better," Ben said, cheerfully.

"Really? Why?" I asked.

Before Ben could answer, I heard the whiny voice of the

Dark Lord, Principal Buthaire, behind me. "Mister Davenport, I dreamt of this moment all summer." Feel free to call him, The Prince of Buttness, if you prefer.

I turned around to see the only one of my three nemeses that had a mustache (as much as my brother, Derek, tried to grow one) standing before me. Ben scurried off without a word. I didn't blame him, although witnesses were always preferred when I was dealing with Principal Buthaire or Randy Warblemacher, my most hated nemesis.

I was confused. "What moment is that, sir?"

"The one where you and I meet exactly as I planned," Principal Buthaire said and then followed it with an evil cackle.

It was too early in the morning for evil cackles. "That's kinda weird, sir."

Principal Buthaire ignored me. "We may have tied last year, but I'm going to win this year. Bigly."

He was lying. We didn't tie last year. I won. Bigly. He did

make my first year of middle school less than enjoyable, but I bested him in every head to head battle.

The Dark Lord continued, "You walk around here like you're Prince Gopher or something, and that ends now." He took a deep breath, seemingly about to continue.

I interrupted, "Is that a real person?" I knew our mascot was a gopher, but I was pretty certain there was no prince attached to the story. I wasn't even sure if there were any gophers in our entire county.

"I don't know," Principal Butt Hair (he claims it's pronounced Boo-tare, but look at the spelling: Buthaire) said, annoyed. "Ask Dr. Dinkledorf. He's the historian. Where was I?"

"You were berating me for no reason, sir."

"Ah, yes. Thank you. You're not middle school royalty no matter how much you parade around here like you are."

I learned enough last year to know that arguing didn't make a difference, so I just kept my mouth shut, which was not always easy for me.

"You may have won Battle of the Bands over the summer, but you will rue the day, rue the day, I say, that you challenged me! I'm the Emperor and you will fall in line or you will find yourself in the dungeon of detention. Consider yourself warned, Mister Davenport," he said in as deep a voice as he could.

"Noted, sir," I said, taking a step back, as we were almost nose to nose as I looked up at him. And a note to self: 7th grade was not going to be better than last year. I would make sure to inform my foolish best friend that his optimism was not warranted.

I saluted him and turned on my heels, eager to get as far away from that lunatic as possible. I headed over toward Sophie, Ditzy Dayna, Ben, and Just Charles.

"Hey," I greeted them all. Sophie and Ditzy Dayna gave me hugs. I wasn't sure Dayna remembered me. She was not exactly the sharpest knife in the drawer.

"Oh, my God!" Sophie yelled excitedly as she looked at the swarm of students pass by.

"What?" I asked. I thought somebody famous was in the building.

"They're so cute. The sixth graders are so tiny."

Ditzy Dayna added in baby talk, "They're wike wittle babies. I just want to pinch their cheeks."

The rest of us laughed.

"We were them last year," Ben said. And then his face went white. "Oh, my Gopher! No. Just no." Ben was looking past us down the hall.

"Dude, are you okay? What did you see?" I thought Ben might faint. And then I saw her. Or it. Technically, she was a girl, but all we saw was a monster walking toward us.

Sophie whisper yelled, "Regan Storm!"

She was the most unlikable of people. She was at Randy Warblemacher level. If you haven't heard about him yet, don't worry. You will. But what was Regan doing at Cherry Avenue? We met her at camp over the summer, but she wasn't in our school the year prior and Sophie had said she was from Bear Creek, which was a different school district.

If anybody was parading around like royalty, it was Regan. But I doubted that Principal Buthaire would ever call her out on it. He gravitated toward idiots like her, my brother, and Randy. Like attracts like, as they say.

Regan walked down the hall announcing herself, "Make way for Regan Storm." She took a menacing step toward a small pack of sixth graders, who all scattered like bugs. Regan threw her head back and laughed.

"What the heck is she doing here?" Ben asked.

"She never said she was moving here when we were at camp," Sophie added.

"Maybe she won't be in any of our classes," I said, hopefully.

"Maybe she got on the wrong bus," Ditzy Dayna said, twirling her hair.

"To the wrong school district?" Ben asked, shaking his head.

Regan spotted us and stopped in front of us, her smirk nearly blocking the hallway. Ben took two steps back.

Regan stared at Sophie. "Morning, ladies."

I wasn't sure if she was referring to Ben, Just Charles, and me as ladies or not, but I wasn't about to ask and put myself in her crosshairs.

Sophie nodded and said in a monotone, "What's up?"

"You seem to be the It girl here, so just wanted to give you a heads up. There's a new queen in town."

Regan gave Sophie a pat on her cheek, smirked, and walked away.

My first day of seventh grade was not going overly well as you already know. History with Dr. Dinkledorf continued that trend. I liked history well enough. And Dr. Dinkledorf was pretty cool for an old dude. He was definitely in my corner in my battle against Principal Buthaire, going so far as to encourage me to break some rules in order to stand up to the oppressive reign of Prince Butt Hair, one of my other pet nicknames for our esteemed principal.

I knew Ben was going to be in our class, so I figured it would be okay. I got to talking with Steven Miley while I waited for Ben to show up. Steven was a good dude, halfway between the nerd and athletic worlds, and nice.

"What'd you do this summer?" Steven asked as we sat at our desks, waiting for the bell to ring.

"My band, Mayhem Mad Men, won Battle of the Bands. What about you?"

"Oh, I played video games. I won Dawn of the Savages. So, about the same as yours."

I couldn't believe he was equating winning a video

game to taking down great bands like Goat Turd and 64 Farts, and of course, Randy Warblemacher's own Love Puddle.

Before I could point out how much more awesome winning Battle of the Bands in real life was to pressing a button to shoot arrows at Neanderthals, history changed forever. Well, not like the history of the world. I was talking more like our history class.

Regan Storm and Randy Warblemacher walked in one after the other.

"Davenfart! I missed your stench!" Randy called out loud enough for the entire class to hear. A bunch of idiots laughed.

Ugh. "Glad to see you're still an immature turd licker, Warblemonster," I said. I got more laughter than he did. I track it on a spreadsheet.

Ben walked in, saw Randy and Regan, and nearly deflated like a fizzled balloon that you accidentally let go before it's tied. The good news was that he didn't make any high-pitched farting sounds, which was a plus.

Ben slipped into the seat next to me, shock still on his face. "We have to endure a whole year of history with not one, but two of those idiots?"

"Seems to be the case," I said, shrugging.

Dr. Dinkledorf stood in front of the class and cleared his throat. "Settle in class. For those of you who don't know me, my name is Dr. Dinkledorf."

"Dinkledork is more like it," Regan whispered.

Dr. Dinkledorf was probably the oldest teacher in the school, so his hearing was a bit less than perfect. He continued on as if he didn't hear Regan's insult, which he probably didn't. "It's going to be a wonderful year. We will begin studying the later medieval period with a specific focus on the Renaissance, one of my favorite topics to explore."

"Snore fest," Randy said.

"And this year, we have a special treat for our seventh graders. A field trip to the medieval town of Chester as it prepares for the 25th anniversary of the Jefferson County Renaissance fair!"

A few small claps echoed through the class room.

Dr. Dinkledorf looked at me with a wide smile. I gave him a thumbs up.

Randy looked over at me and mouthed, "Dork."

Dr. Dinkledorf said, "Permission slips are due by the end of the week."

THANKFULLY, I had third period with Sophie, Ben, and Sammie, and no Randy or Regan. I sat with them at lunch. There's nothing like school lunch at ten o'clock in the morning. And it looked like they started the year off with a bang. Ham loaf. Don't know what ham loaf is? You might not want to. But I'll tell you just in case. It's meat loaf, but with ham.

Look, nobody's expecting lobster thermidor for three dollars, but ham loaf on the first day? It was like they didn't care enough to even pretend it was going to be a good year. Everybody knows that most parents only ask about how school went on the first day. You tell them it went great because you have no homework and they served pizza and everybody's happy. But no, they couldn't even give us that.

I ate a bunch of corn as we chatted. Sammie was going on and on about cheerleading tryouts, which was kinda boring, so I just wondered what the point was of even eating corn when it comes out looking exactly like it did on the way in.

"I'm so nervous," Sammie said, playing with her food.

"Is that why you're not eating the ham loaf?" Ben asked with a smile.

That's why he's my best friend.

"Sophie," Sammie said, "I still can't believe you don't want to be a cheerleader. I wish you would've tried out with me."

Sophie shrugged. "It's not my thing. Hopefully, you and Dayna will make the team together."

I couldn't imagine Ditzy Dayna remembering any of the cheers, but I didn't want to dash any of Sammie's hopes.

"We find out today after school. Tryouts were two weeks long! I learned so much. I can't wait."

THE FINAL BELL rang throughout the school. Kids cheered like we had just survived a 12-round boxing match with the heavyweight champ. I'm not a boxing fan, but I'm pretty certain whoever the heavyweight champ was couldn't handle a day of middle school. I gathered my books and backpack at my locker. I heard footsteps stomping behind me.

"You're never gonna believe this!" Sammie said, annoyed.

"What?" I asked. I had a feeling she was going to tell me even if I didn't want to know.

"Regan Storm made the team! She didn't even try out!"

"She probably beat up your coach or pushed her into the pool or something." Maybe I was just bitter. She pushed Ben and me into the pool at summer camp. She totally caught me by surprise and I'm certain that she works out with a trainer. "Do you know how you did?"

"Oh, yeah. I made the team," she said, nonchalantly.

"Great! Just be happy that you made it. I'm happy for you."

"It is so exciting," she said, jumping up and down. She didn't have any pom poms, but she was already looking the part of a cheerleader.

"Don't forget that we've been friends for basically our whole lives. Now that you're really cool, I'm just worried you're going to forget about me. Or worse."

Sammie pushed me, playfully. "Don't worry, dummy. Cheerleaders and dweebs can be friends."

"See? It's starting already," I said with raised eyebrows.

"I'm just kidding," Sammie said.

I hoped so, but I had seen it before. When nerds and other non-popular kids get accepted into the popular group, a lot of them change.

IT WAS the first football game of the season, so the whole world stopped so we could worship the royalty of smelly kids with anger issues running in strange patterns across some finely-cut grass. Or maybe I just don't get it.

Perhaps you noticed. I don't really care about football. Sometimes, the strategy of it all was cool, but overall, I wasn't impressed. My dad always tried to get me to understand it. He loved football and watching Derek play it well. My mom was more the intellectual like me and didn't really know what was going on. Either Derek ran far with the ball, which was good, or he didn't run far with it, which was bad.

I sat in the stands with my parents and Sophie. The

game was tied late in the fourth quarter and the fearsome Gophers had the ball against the Brighton Bisons.

My dad leaned over to me and Sophie and said, "Mr. Muscalini loves the 44 Blast. He's gonna call it once we get closer."

"What the heck is the 44 Blast?" I asked.

"It's a running play where the fullback leads the way, blasting through the line, opening a hole for the running back."

I understood what he was talking about, but I also found it kinda boring, so I imagined that instead the fullback blasted a worm hole into the core of the universe that Derek ran into and disappeared from, en route to another galaxy. What? Just some brotherly love.

"Got that?" I asked Sophie.

"Yep, Nick is gonna punch a hole in the line. Randy will hand off to Derek, who will follow Nick."

"She's a keeper," my dad said.

Sophie understood it more than I did. I smiled. "She is, but not because of her football knowledge."

Sophie and I both blushed. I rarely saw her embarrassed. I was usually embarrassing myself enough for both of us.

The Gophers lined up against the Bisons, threatening to score from about ten yards out of the end zone. Randy stood behind center as the quarterback with Derek behind him as the running back and the gargantuan Nick DeRozan next to Derek as the fullback.

"Here it comes," my dad said, "44 Blast."

"If you know it's coming, don't they know it's coming?" That's at least something I could get my brain around. It's called game theory. It's super interesting. It analyzes competitive situations where the outcome of one player/participant is dependent on the choices of others. Sorry for the nerd diversion.

My dad answered, "Maybe, but with Nick blasting the hole and your brother's speed, it probably doesn't matter."

I secretly hoped that Brighton did know it was coming and rooted for Randy to get run over by a herd of Bison. Derek getting run over would be a close second on my wish list. You may find that a bit harsh, but Randy deserved a few herds worth of a trampling, and my brother at least a few stomps.

The team broke from the huddle and lined up in front of the Bisons. Randy yelled out, "Gopher 22! I wear pink underwear! I'm a dummy and can't ride a bike!" At least that's what it sounded like with his mouthpiece in.

Randy received the ball from the monster in front of him and turned to Nick DeRozan. He faked a handoff to Nick, who was lumbering to the hoard of clashing Neanderthals. Nick blasted two incoming Bison like he was swatting flies, as Randy handed the ball to Derek, who followed a few steps behind Nick. Dudes were flying everywhere like pins in a bowling alley. Derek ran untouched, spun around a defender and into the end zone for a touchdown.

The crowd went nuts. My parents jumped up, cheering. My dad looked down at me and lightly slapped my shoulder. "See? 44 Blast gets it done every time."

I clapped a few times just so nobody thought I was too weird. It was like if you didn't like football, you had something wrong with you.

Derek ran to the sideline holding the football over his head as his teammates mobbed him. He broke free from the crowd as he passed by the bouncing cheerleaders and flipped the ball to Sammie, who was shaking her pom poms wildly. She stopped dead in her tracks, frozen. The ball hit her in the head and bounced across the ground. Regan stood next to her and laughed. Sammie's brain unfroze and when she realized what had just happened, she thrust her pom poms in the air and kicked her leg exuberantly, her shin touching her shoulder, and unfortunately (or fortunately, depending on how you look at it) kicked Regan in the face. Regan fell to the floor, holding her nose. I couldn't wait to thank Sammie for that.

The 44 Blast, which resulted in Derek's touchdown, was the difference in the game. The mighty Gophers stomped the Bisons 21-14. And everybody was running around like world hunger had been solved because a bunch of middle schoolers ran across a line three times holding an oddly-shaped ball.

∼

AFTER THE GAME, we hung out in the atrium of the school. We waited for Mr. Muscalini to give a motivational speech or whatever he does after games and for Derek to change.

The cheerleaders came out first. Some of them acknowledged Sophie, but the entire pack of girls ignored me, which was the norm. Cheerleaders and Nerd Nation were like caviar and bottled farts. They might both smell terrible, but the caviar people thought they were so much better. That's why I was afraid that Sammie would go over to the Dark Side. She was a bottled farts girl through and through. It would crush me if she joined the caviar crowd.

And then Regan came out, an ice pack on her nose, mumbling about Sammie to Veronica Moore. "She shouldn't even be on the team! She doesn't know what she's doing."

I couldn't help myself. "Lookin' good, Regan," I said, smiling.

She didn't even realize I was making fun of her. "In your dreams, dork!"

Sophie looked at me and said, annoyed, "Really?"

"I was kidding," I said. "She looked like an idiot." I shook my head.

The doors burst open and Randy walked out. He walked toward us, all fake smiles to my parents. "Mr. And Mrs. Davenport, so wonderful to see you again. I often tell my mother how much I enjoyed Thanksgiving at your house last year."

My parents knew better than to fall for his nonsense again. They knew everything I had been through with him.

"We're so glad you enjoyed it," my mother said. "Please give your parents our best."

My dad was more enthused, more so about the game.

"Great work out there, Randy. That hook and ladder and oh, the flea flicker. And of course, the 44 Blast."

Randy beamed as he walked by. "Thanks," he said to my dad.

As he passed me, Randy leaned in and whispered in my ear, "I'm gonna get you, Davenfart. The moment you least expect it."

"What if I always expect it equally?"

"Your snark won't save you, Davenfart. Even if you see me coming. I'm like the 44 Blast. Gonna run right over you. Kinda like when you and I played basketball, one on one."

Gulp. I forgot about that. Or the concussion caused me to. I can't remember.

3

It was time for the class trip to Chester, the medieval replica town. Dr. Dinkledorf was probably the most excited out of all of us and he practically lived there. Not only was he a crazy history buff, but he was also head of the Jefferson County Historical Society and an honorary Lord of Chester.

We arrived at Thomas Jefferson County Park, home of the year-round medieval town of Chester. I hadn't been there in about a year. It was where we learned about how much it stunk to live in the 1500s. Chester was also the host of the annual Renaissance fair, which was pretty cool for us nerds. I had attended a few times with my family.

Once we got off the buses, we walked straight into the town. We were greeted by all of the working members of the town: the blacksmith, millers, bakers, the tailor, and others. Dr. Dinkledorf gathered us in the town's center that was surrounded by a dozen shops with thatched roofs. It also had an elevated stage area that had five empty stockades meant for prisoners. My mother took a picture of me, Derek, and Leighton in them a few years ago.

Dr. Dinkledorf addressed us from atop the stage. We stood in a giant group in front of him. I was with Sophie, Sammie, Ben, Just Charles, and Luke. I know, what else is new?

He said, "The Renaissance period was fueled by two important events: the fall of Constantinople, which led to the migration of Greeks into Italy, taking their texts and ideas with them, and the introduction of the printing press to Europe, which led to the rapid spread of new ideas."

Regan said in rapid succession, "Snore. Snore. Snore. Snore. Snore. Snore."

Of course, all of the kiss-ups and wannabe popular kids laughed.

Dr. Dinkledorf continued, "As if that's not exciting enough, I'm going to let you in on a little secret sneak peak of what's coming in a few weeks at this year's Renaissance festival. Being the twenty-fifth anniversary of the festival, we will be naming a prince and princess of The Realm! But this won't simply be handed to a handsome or pretty face, oh no! The victors will have to complete a quest! Should you be 12 years of age and under and your parents sign a lengthy waiver, you can enter and prove your worth to the Protectors of the Realm!"

Ditzy Dayna jumped up and down and asked, "I love the Renaissance fair! Will there be unicorns there this year? They never have them. I've always wanted to ride one."

Dr. Dinkledorf looked at her with pity. "Not this year, sweetie."

"Even on the twenty-fifth anniversary?" Ditzy Dayna whined.

"I'm afraid not," Dr. Dinkledorf said.

Randy asked, "What's the big deal? I mean why should we care about the Renaissance period?"

"Good question, Mr. Warblemacher," Dr. Dinkledorf said, while pacing across the stage. "It brought about the art of Leonardo, Michelangelo, Raphael."

Regan chimed in, "The Renaissance period gave us the Ninja Turtles?"

Dr. Dinkledorf shook his head and continued, "It also gave us literature like Chaucer and Shakespeare." He looked at us expectantly.

Everybody stared. It was not the response Dr. Dinkledorf expected.

"The Renaissance period gave us buttons," Dr. Dinkledorf said, seemingly exhausted and drained of all enthusiasm and will to live. "Without the Renaissance period, you would not have buttons."

"Oh, sweet," Cheryl Van Snoogle-Something said.

"That sounds pretty awesome," Sammie said.

"I love buttons," Nick DeRozan said in his man voice.

Dr. Dinkledorf took a deep breath and looked up at the sky. "I think I need to retire. Please send me a sign. Or was this the sign?"

I raised my hand and asked, "Sir, surely there were other cool things about the medieval and renaissance periods besides buttons, like knights and stuff?"

"Oh, yes. Thank you, Mr. Davenport."

Randy looked over at me and called out, "Kiss up. Why don't you just go up there and kiss his old, wrinkly butt?" Randy didn't normally speak that way in front of teachers. He was more of a kiss up than anyone, but he was emboldened by Dr. Dinkledorf's terrible hearing.

I shook my head and focused on Dr. Dinkledorf as he continued, "The later medieval time period was a very exciting time. Knights lay siege to castles with catapults and jousted in tournaments for gold and glory. It was a time of princes and princesses, kings and queens."

Dr. Dinkledorf was interrupted by Kieran Murphy who pointed and yelled, "Who is that? That guy is totally wicked."

Kieran was pointing to a man walking in the distance. He wore a long shaggy, brown beard, a dark cloak, big boots, and a sword strapped to his waist.

Dr. Dinkledorf smiled. "That is Thaddeus Dinkledorf, Lord of the Dragons, high protector of The Realm."

"Dinkledorf?" Kieran asked.

"Yes, he is my son. Heir to the Dinkledorf throne," Dr. Dinkledorf said, dramatically.

"Why is he dressed up for the fair already?" Cheryl Van Snoogle-Something asked.

"That is how he always dresses. Thaddeus is also our Quest Master. He and his team are hard at work designing the royal quest. Should you be of noble heart, strong in mind and body, and be okay with wearing a tunic in front of others, perhaps you will be the winner..."

Sophie looked at me and whispered, "I've always wanted to be a princess. That sounds like fun."

Not really. I mean, I'd love to be a prince and have Sophie as my princess, but my legs were not strong nor would they look good dangling from the bottom of a tunic. I wasn't exactly the quest type, unless it involved computers or science and I was pretty certain that wouldn't be the case. So, I just nodded and smiled.

Sophie grabbed my hand. My heart nearly stopped. She asked, "Would you like to go with me, you know, as a date?"

I couldn't say no to a date with Sophie. I looked at her and said, "As long as I don't have to wear a tunic, I'm in."

"But you have to. Are you going to stand there in jeans while I wear a fair maiden's dress?"

"Yes?"

4

I was pumped that I had a date set with Sophie at the Renaissance fair. I was less pumped that my wardrobe was still open to debate and it was leaning toward tunic, which, if you don't know what that is, close your ears while I tell you. It's basically a dress that dudes wore, but with a belt. It was all the rage 500 years ago. Today? Not so much.

The rest of the day was not overly exciting. We milked a cow and churned some butter, but besides that, there was not a whole lot to do except watch the blacksmith make stuff. And that got kinda boring after like three minutes, because all it entailed was watching stuff get hot in the fire and then him hitting it with a hammer over and over and over again.

It was not overly exciting, until that is, my epic sword battle with Randy. I was standing with Ben and Just Charles when I heard Randy whisper in my ear, "Having fun, peasant?"

I turned around. "I was until you showed up," I said, turning my back on him.

Randy shoved me lightly from behind, more to get a rise from me than to knock me over. "Don't turn your back on me."

I walked away as I said, "Dude, just get away from me."

Everything settled down for a few minutes until I heard Randy call from behind me, "Heads up, Davenfart!"

I turned around to see a wooden sword flying through the air toward me and Randy with a sword, heading my way. Of course, it was the first time I ever caught something in my life. I was about to throw it back at him, but it was kind of heavy, and oh, Randy was charging me. I gripped the sword by the handle, fear surging through my body as Randy sliced the sword through the air toward my shoulder.

Somehow, my sword found its way to Randy's and blocked it with a smack.

"Dude, knock it off," I said, steadying my sword in case he struck again.

"Never. You think last year was hard? I was just getting warmed up."

Oh, great.

Randy surged forward, swinging the sword wildly. I blocked the first attack, but he connected with a second. My shoulder surged with pain. I stepped back and looked around. The entire seventh grade encircled us, of course with no adults anywhere in sight.

"You'll never be better than me at anything, Davenfart. I always win."

"I kinda remember you cheating a whole lot in pretty much everything we've ever competed against each other in. You wouldn't be so tough to beat if you actually followed the rules."

"Oh, you think you're tougher than me? You wouldn't last a day in medieval times," Randy said with a laugh.

"I love going to Medieval Times. You eat with your hands. They joust. It's a lot of fun."

"Shut up, Davenfart. It's time to talk with our swords."

Before I could come up with a clever retort, Randy was headed toward me again, sword swinging.

I blocked one attack and dodged another, but it left Randy more beside me than in front of me with my sword on the wrong side of us. I turned and ran. Randy chased me in a circle, whacking me as I ran. In hindsight, it was not the best of strategies.

I stumbled over my own feet and then a pail that lay on its side next to the water well. A bunch of kids laughed.

Sophie rushed out of the crowd and in between me and Randy. She pushed him as hard as she could with both hands. He was nearly a head taller than her (and me), so he barely budged. Randy laughed and pushed Sophie to the side. She fell to the ground in a puff of dirt.

Now, I was angry. I stood up as quickly as I could and ran toward Randy. I drew the sword back behind my head and let out a medieval scream, as I sliced the sword down diagonally toward his hip.

Randy jutted his waist backward, avoiding my massive blow. The momentum of my monstrous attack carried me forward and spun my back away from Randy. I ended up in the less-than-desirable position of having my vicious opponent directly behind me. Randy wrapped his arms around me, picked me up, and carried me toward a giant barrel that doubled as a garbage can.

I kicked and squirmed and said really ferocious things like, "Get off of me, you jerk!" and "Stop it, idiot!"

Despite my witty and persuasive argument, Randy dumped me into the garbage can with a laugh. I was at least thankful that I went butt first and not face first.

The crowd laughed again. Randy walked away smirking. He handed the sword to Ava Sasser, who giggled like a movie star just kissed her or something. I mentally crossed her name off my holiday card list. Not sure why that was the first thought that came to mind as I sat stuck in the garbage, but it was.

Seventh grade. Like sixth grade. Only worse.

5
___

Regan rushed up to Randy as he walked away from me. She looked at him like he just won the Super Bowl.

She said, "You're so cool. Randy. We're going out again."

They had dated briefly over the summer when we were all at Camp Cherriwacka together. She dumped him after he was too flirty with some of his fans when he was the lead singer of the band, Love Puddle. I know, ridiculous name, right?

"Good, I've been telling everyone that we were getting back together anyway," Randy said seriously.

"I like your confidence," Regan said through a wicked smile.

Ben and Just Charles hurried over to me and tried to pull me out. Sophie and Sammie were right behind them. Ben and Just Charles' kindergarten-level strength was not adequate. Thaddeus Dinkledorf caught my eye and rushed over to me. I took the hand he offered me. With one pull, the burly knight ripped me from the pail with a strange suction sound.

"Find yourself on the wrong end of a melee, did we, young sir?"

"I don't know what any of that means. I just got my butt kicked and I want him to leave me alone."

Thaddeus shaped his long beard with one hand while the other rested on the hilt of his sword. "Once a warrior tastes blood, his thirst for it grows. If you desire peace, young nobleman, you must go to war."

"That doesn't make any sense."

"Doesn't it?" Thaddeus asked.

"The only war we're good at is a war of words," Ben said.

"And even then, we still take a lot of insults," Just Charles added.

Thaddeus shook his head. "You can hide from or deflect your troubles, young sir, but they'll always be lurking in the shadows like a Florentine assassin! But face your troubles head on and you shall vanquish them!"

He patted me on the shoulder with such strength that I almost preferred he tossed me back into the garbage pail. Head first.

I smiled through the pain. "Thank you, sir. I will take that under advisement."

He wasn't finished with his speech. He was like a medieval Mr. Muscalini. "Valor in the face of tyranny shall release you from your internal prison, no matter the outcome!"

"Even if you end up in a garbage pail?" I asked.

"Especially when you end up in a garbage pail," Thaddeus said with another clap of my shoulder. "Fare thee well, young nobles. I bid you adieu." He leaned into me and said, "I gotta go make a do-do." Thaddeus looked at Sophie and Sammie and said, "My ladies, be well."

After Thaddeus was out of ear shot, I let out a manly

whimper and said, "Does anybody know what he was talking about?"

"He thinks you should stand up to Randy," Sophie said. "Not sure what he was talking about with the garbage pail."

"Yeah, that was a low point," Just Charles said.

"I just stood up to him and lost," I said, frustrated. "I could've run away, but I fought."

"Well, you did run for a minute there. I mean, your definition of running," Ben said, unhelpfully.

"I'm just so mad. I don't know what to do about Randy," Sophie said, crossing her arms.

"And now we have Regan to deal with, too," Sammie said. "She's been bashing me ever since I kicked her in the face."

"Nice work on that, by the way," I said.

"It was an accident," Sammie said, defensively.

I looked at Sophie and said, "Just let it go. You can't win with him. I'm just gonna have to take whatever he gives me."

"It's not about winning," Sophie said, seething. "It's about what's right."

Sophie turned and stormed toward Randy, even angrier than when she thought I kissed Zoey Hicks last year.

As she headed toward Randy, she yelled, "What is wrong with you?"

Randy smirked. "I stopped listening to anything you had to say after we broke up."

"You mean when I dumped you?"

"It didn't happen that way," Randy scoffed.

"Keep telling yourself that."

"I'm the quarterback. Girls don't break up with me."

"Didn't Regan break up with you during the summer? I remember you crying like a baby on stage at one of your performances."

"You saw that?" Randy asked, surprised, and then, "I don't remember that even happening."

"Just stay away from us," Sophie spat. She turned her back on Randy and walked back toward us.

She looked at me and said, "You're right. You can't win with him."

Derek walked over toward us, well, to Sammie. Her face lit up.

I didn't care. I stepped in between the two of them. "Where were you, Derek? You're the worst brother in the world."

"How is you getting beat up my fault? I didn't do it."

"Yeah, you didn't do anything."

6

A s we waited for the buses (or time-travel vessels as Dr. Dinkledorf called them), Just Charles shook his head and said, "You should complain to the principal."

I looked at him and smirked. "Really, dude? You think Butt Hair cares about me getting beat up? He probably ordered the attack."

Ben said, "He's right. This is getting ridiculous. You need to tell your parents."

"No," I said, firmly. "I don't want to be the kid who tattled."

"Why not?" Sophie asked. "This has to stop. He went too far this time. I'll say something. He pushed me to the ground."

Luke ignored Sophie and said, "You gotta drop the gauntlet! Remember what Thaddeus said? If you want peace, you must go to war!"

"I thought we said that was stupid?" I asked.

"Did we? I thought it was kinda cool," Luke said,

scratching his head. "I was pretty amped up about all the vanquishing he was going on about."

I looked around at my crew. "Guys, look. I know you're looking out for me. Getting Randy suspended isn't going to stop him. Did you ever meet his parents? There's a reason he is the way he is. Getting him in trouble will just make it worse. I can't win by tattle. I have to beat Randy in epic fashion."

But how? I had no idea. It had to be something I could actually beat him at, even if he tried to cheat. The answer to that mystery was nothing. There was nothing I could beat Randy at besides Battle of the Bands. And I just beat him in Battle of the Bands a few weeks ago and it didn't deter him at all. Maybe it just made him angrier. I'm convinced I could crush him in chess and solving math problems like inequalities or graphing linear equations, but that didn't exactly give you street cred.

"Any ideas? Now would be a good time," Ben said.

I looked around at everyone. Nobody had anything. Or seemingly any confidence in my ability to beat Randy at anything. I didn't blame them. And then an idea popped into my head. A good one. The best, actually.

"Do you know what would be an epic takedown?"

"What?"

"Beating Randy in the quest."

Ben nodded and said, "Yeah, it would." Then he looked at me, 'Wait, you're serious?"

I looked at the entire crew. "I need to take him down in the quest. There's no other way. You need to turn me into a knight."

7

I was already the laughingstock of school. My new nickname was "The Garbage Pail Peasant." I was pretty sure that Randy and Regan were behind that. I figured it couldn't get any worse. I had nothing to lose. I had my friends and they weren't going anywhere. But Randy had everything to lose. He was the quarterback of the football team and the most popular kid in school, mainly because of all the girls. Most dudes who didn't play sports with him, and even some of his teammates, didn't like him.

As much as I knew my friends would always be there for me, they also weren't overly supportive about my decision to take Randy down in the quest. I didn't blame them. Turning me into a knight was a tall order. I'm not even sure if Harry Potter had a spell that powerful.

I needed three things to happen. First, I needed to challenge Randy in public so that he had to accept. I was worried that he wouldn't even want to waste his energy on me. Second, I needed to transform into Sir Austin Davenport the Destroyer. I had no idea how that was going to happen without Harry Potter, so I decided to leave that one to Ben and Just Charles to figure out. And finally, I had to crush Randy in the quest. He was strong, fast, smart, and he cheated better than he did anything else.

If you remember from any of my previous adventures, getting called down to Principal Buthaire's office via the Speaker of Doom was basically a weekly occurrence. A tradition that continued into seventh grade. It wasn't because I was badly behaved. I was one of the best students in the school and got along with all my teachers and most of the kids that weren't idiots. Principal Buthaire just had it out for me. Hey, you can't be short, nerdy, need glasses for long distances, wear braces, and have the principal like you all at the same time. That wouldn't be fair to anyone.

So, as I sat in the main office, waiting for Principal Butt Hair to make up some ridiculous reason for giving me detention and a thought occurred to me. Typically, I'm not all that impulsive. I like to plan things out, but with the opportunity right in front of me for the taking, I struck like a duck. You probably haven't heard that saying before, but it's really popular in aquatic circles.

I looked up at the clock to see that there were still eight minutes left in Advisory before the first period bell rang. And morning announcements hadn't begun. Cheryl Van Snoogle-Something waved to me as she stood next to Mrs. Murphy, one of the office secretaries. It was Cheryl's turn to do the student announcements into the Speaker of Doom.

Mrs. Murphy said, "Just push this button, dear, and then you can read the announcements."

"Okay," Cheryl said, her voice shaking. She took a deep breath and pushed the button. "Good morning. Today's lunch options are Jello Chicken..." Cheryl paused, seemingly throwing up in her mouth. "Tuna and salmon casserole," Cheryl continued with her eyes closed. "And for dessert, black licorice sorbet."

Cheryl turned around toward Mrs. Murphy and me. Her face was white as a ghost. She held both her stomach and her mouth as she ran toward the door. "I think I'm gonna be sick."

Mrs. Murphy followed her into the hallway. My eyes widened at the opportunity before me. The main office was empty. The Butt Crack's door was closed. That's what I named Principal Butt Hair's office. His name was Butt Hair and he was a butt crack. It didn't take my genius-level intellect to come up with that one. And the entire school sat in rapt attention, waiting for the next batch of morning announcements.

I stepped up to the Speaker of Doom, the sense of power that Principal Butt Hair must've felt, surged through my body. I smiled to myself and pressed the button.

"We interrupt this regularly-scheduled programming for this special announcement. Randolph Nancy Warblemacher, I, Austin Davenport, hereby challenge your cheating butt to a battle, a medieval quest to be exact."

The Butt Crack flew open, shaking the walls.

"Davenport!" Principal Buthaire screamed at the top of his lungs. I think a few of the pictures on the wall rattled. "In my office, now!"

I leaned into the microphone and said, "Let me know! Gotta go, now. Bye!"

Even though I knew I was in a lot of trouble, I was pumped. For once, I used the Speaker of Doom to my advantage. For perhaps just a touch more than once, I actually deserved the detention I received.

My meeting with Principal Buthaire began. I sat in The

Butt Crack in front of his desk as he stared back at me through his glasses with his beady eyes.

"MISTERRRRRRRRRRR DAVENPORT," Principal Buthaire said, for some reason holding the 'r' longer than normal. "Our beginning-of-the-year talk apparently didn't get through to you, because here we stand."

We were both sitting, but I didn't think pointing that out would help the situation.

Principal Butt Hair licked his fingers and straightened his mustache. It was pretty gross, but again, not something to point out. He continued, "Of course, you will receive detention for the morning announcement stunt. But you also get this promise. I'm going to make life very difficult for you. Wherever you are, I'll be, handing you a detention slip for the rule you surely just broke. In the cafeteria, oh, hello, Misterrrrrr Davenport. Insulting Mrs. Jenkins' fine passion-fruit pudding? (I called it passionpuke.) Detention. Horsing around in the locker room? I'll be there watching and holding a detention slip."

"Sir, you probably shouldn't hang out in the kids' locker room watching us change," I said.

Principal Buthaire shook his head. "You're even dumber than I thought. You just never learn. You flout my authority at every turn, even when the consequences keep getting worse."

Perhaps I was dumber than I thought, too, because I had no idea what flout meant. Or maybe it was the word that was dumb.

He continued, "You're going to pay, Misterrrrr Davenport."

"I don't have a job, sir."

"That's an extra day's detention for you. Oh, don't like that? Make it two. No, three." He looked at me and smiled. "Why squabble over a detention here and there? Let's make it a week. And from now on, I will only hand out detentions to you in weekly increments. Think twice before you mess with the Speaker of Doom," Principal Butt Hair, said in his deepest voice possible.

~

I WALKED into the cafeteria to a few claps, a few hundred sympathetic looks, and Sophie's beautiful eyes bulging at me.

"What did you do?" Sophie asked.

"I made a huge mistake," I said.

"How much detention did you get?" Sophie asked, concerned.

"A lot, but I wasn't talking about that. With the way everyone is looking at me, it appears as if I just signed my own death warrant. Death by quest."

"Think positive," she said.

I nodded. "I'm positively going to get crushed."

Ben and Sammie walked up behind me and slid into their seats.

"What did you do?" Sammie asked.

I couldn't go through the whole thing again. I furrowed my brow and asked, "What are you talking about?"

"How can you beat him?" Sammie asked.

"That seems to be the question of the day. I just read my obituary in the school newspaper." I looked at Ben and said, "I hope you know what you're doing."

"With what?" he asked.

Oh, boy. I was in serious trouble. I was starting to get the feeling he had never trained a knight before.

It was time for knight training. Ben, Just Charles, Luke, and I gathered in my backyard on a sunny September Saturday. None of us had ever trained a knight before or knew anyone who had, so we kind-of just winged it.

Ben asked the group, "What are the skills and traits that Austin needs to acquire?"

"Fifty pounds of muscle," Luke answered, unhelpfully.

"Funny," I said, less than enthused.

"Mr. Muscalini can get that done in no time," Just Charles said, laughing.

"Seriously, guys. What can we do?" I asked.

"Well, your sword fighting certainly needs improvement," Ben said.

"Agreed," I said, remembering my lost battle with Randy that ended with me in a garbage can. "Thanks for crushing my spirit before training even started."

"Sorry, but don't take it personally. This is all constructive. All of us would need serious work to beat Randy, if that's even possible."

I was starting to believe it wasn't. Or already did.

"So, sword, and I would say jousting. And just general toughness," Just Charles said.

"That's a good starting point," Luke said. "I think we should start by bashing your fingers with a hammer. Do you know how much that hurts?"

"Umm, we're not doing that," I said. "What time is your mother picking you up?" I asked.

"I don't know. Why?"

"No reason," I said. I paced around in a circle. "Well, knights have armor, swords, and horses. Did you bring any of those?"

"Can't say that we did," Ben said, as we all thought.

"My horse is out of town," Just Charles said.

"I finally figured out what Derek is good for!" I yelled.

"What?" the group asked.

"Borrowing used sports equipment from him." Our shed, garage, and basement were like a smorgasbord of sporting goods. Now I know why my Dad always says we can't go on vacation anywhere nice. He spent all of our money on stuff to protect Derek from balls whizzing through the air. I'm pretty certain the money could've been better spent. We were going to Mexico in less than two months, our first big vacation in like forever. My mom is obsessed with Dia de Los Muertos, the Day of the Dead. I'll tell you about that another time.

"Let's hit the garage first," I said, waving for the crew to follow me.

We entered the garage through the back door. I flipped on the lights, revealing a bunch of my dad's tools and what appeared to be a used sports equipment store. Every piece of protective gear and ball you could think of was there from baseball, football, hockey, golf, basketball, and soccer. The only things I didn't see were a quaffle and the golden snitch from Quiddich. My brother was definitely not wizard material, unless Slytherin would have him.

"Oh, my word," Just Charles said.

"I don't even know what all this stuff does," Ben said.

"We need armor," I said.

Luke grabbed a catcher's chest protector while Ben and Just Charles grabbed the shin guards and the mask. I slipped on some hockey gloves.

"This oughta work," Luke said.

"Weapons," Ben said, scanning the walls and over-flowing bins.

I grabbed three hockey sticks while Luke picked up a baseball bat.

"Whoa, dude. We won't be needing that just yet," I said. No need to get crazy on the first day of training.

Luke put the bat down with a clank and a look of disappointment on his face.

Ben looked at me and said, "Suit up, Cinderella. We're your fairy godmothers."

"Please don't ever call me that again," I said. "It's bad enough to be insulted by Randy. I don't need you doing it, too."

"Yeah, I want no part of any of that," Luke said.

"Yep, bad call on my part. Let's get going."

We walked back out into the yard. I strapped on the catcher's gear. Ben handed a hockey stick to Luke, Just Charles, and me.

Ben said, "One at a time, swing at half speed. Just practice blocking from side to side. And then we'll speed things up."

I liked Ben making up the training plan. I knew he wouldn't try to get me killed. I didn't like Luke with a hockey stick in his hand with the go-ahead to start whacking me with it, but I at least had a ton of protection.

"Are you readyeth to become a knight?" Ben asked with enthusiasm, raising his fist in the air.

"Yes," I said, with less enthusiasm. I held the hockey stick with the hockey blade below my hands, using the wooden handle as the sword blade.

Ben looked at Just Charles and nodded. "Begin!"

Just Charles stepped forward and swung the long

hockey stick slowly. I had plenty of time to block it. Our sticks clashed with a thwack. I looked over at Luke, who had already begun swinging his stick at me with fury in his eyes. I stepped to the side and blocked it. Just Charles let out a scream and attacked twice as fast and hard at the first. I parried the blow while Luke also sped up his attack.

Luke's stick caught me on the shoulder as I was too slow to block it, which set off a chain reaction that I'd rather not relive, but is an important part of the story, so I'll tell you. I winced in pain, causing me to miss the block on Just Charles' attack. It knocked me back toward Luke, who smacked me again, and turned my training into a hockey game with me as the puck.

Luke let out a primal scream and cracked the stick over my helmeted head.

I fell to the ground like a Jenga game gone wrong, the chest protector cushioning the blow, but not enough to keep the wind from getting knocked out of me. I really could've done without it. I pulled off the catcher's mask and dropped it on the grass. I didn't have words. I barely had air.

"That felt good!" Luke yelled.

Just Charles threw his fist in the air and yelled, "Huzzah!"

"God bless you," I groaned.

"I didn't sneeze. That's a medieval cheer of excitement."

"Oh, great. I'm ecstatic," I said, sounding anything but ecstatic. I was feeling more like I was going to puke so maybe 'Hwulah' was more like it.

"Sorry, got caught up in the moment."

"I don't feel like a knight. I feel more like a peasant," I said, forcing myself to my knees.

"Really? I thought that went rather well," Ben said.

I whispered through pain, "You're fired. I'd rather Randy

dump me in a garbage can. Or in the Great Pit of Carkoon so that I may be digested over centuries by the Sarlacc." The same fate as Boba Fett from Star Wars.

I heard the back door to the house open and then footsteps walking toward us.

"What are you nerds doing?" Derek asked, confused. "Did you break any of my stuff?"

I stood up and said, "We didn't break anything and you outgrew most of this stuff a year ago. Do you happen to have a first aid kit in there? Asking for a friend."

"Yeah, right. Forgot you were such a runt. But seriously, what the heck are you doing?" Derek asked, amused.

"Training for the quest. I've got to take down Randy."

"That's a tall order, little bro," Derek said, chuckling. "I could probably beat him, though." Derek thought about it for a moment. "Yeah, I'll join in on the competition. Thanks for the invite. This is a date situation thing, right? Maybe I'll ask Sammie."

Derek shrugged, turned, and left.

"Who invited him?" I asked.

8

On Monday after history class, Dr. Dinkledorf called me over for a quick chat. I waited for the class to empty before walking up toward his desk. Just the idea of bumping into someone with my level of soreness hurt.

"You okay?" Dr. Dinkledorf asked, as he watched me walk gingerly toward him.

I gave him a thumbs up. "Fabulous. I feel like a million years old."

"I know how you feel. I'm only half a million," he said with a smile.

"Training," I said with a grunt. "Ben's trying to turn me into a knight."

"Glad you're taking the quest seriously. Mr. Warblemacher will be a formidable challenger. I was telling the other Protectors about the courage you showed."

"Protectors, sir?"

"Of The Realm. It is a council of sorts, made up of a few members of the Historical Society and a few guests of my choosing. I've asked Mr. Gifford and Zorch to join us in this year's festivities. They've served in years past."

"What about Mr. Muscalini? I'm sure he would want to put on some sort of feats of strength show for the crowd?"

Dr. Dinkledorf laughed heartily. "Actually, he wants to be the jester."

"Really?" The idea of Mr. Muscalini as the jester didn't make any sense. True, he was very funny, but most of the time, he didn't mean to be.

"One thing you should be prepared for is the Presentation of the Rose ceremony. I think a certain young lady might appreciate you putting a little thought into it," Dr. Dinkledorf said with a smile.

"Rose ceremony?" I asked.

"Yes. As you know, the quest is for two partners. Before the quest begins, each boy will present his potential princess with a rose. Her acceptance signifies their partnership. Some just give the rose. Most of the boys are embarrassed, to be honest. Other presentations are more elaborate. It depends on the relationship. I'm sure Sophie would appreciate a noble gesture. And should the Protectors' decision prove to be a difficult one, the Rose ceremony could sway them. I mean, if you don't get an arrow to the forehead or anything."

"We're going to shoot arrows at each other?" I asked, horrified.

"No. Nothing of the sort. Just a little joke. Sorry, I'll leave those to Mr. Muscalini."

I took a deep breath and exhaled.

"Good luck," Dr. Dinkledorf said as he clapped my shoulder.

A part of me died, as I groaned, still in pain from the training session.

I SAT WITH SOPHIE, Ben, and Sammie at lunch. One would think you couldn't go wrong with mac n cheese, but that one would be wrong. It was green. And it wasn't St. Patrick's Day.

"What is this?" I asked.

"Why does it look like an art project gone bad?" Sophie asked.

"I think mine moved," Sammie said.

"It's not stho bad," Ben said with an unhealthy helping of the green goop in his mouth.

"And we wonder why Ben doesn't have a girlfriend," I said with a smile.

"That hurts," he said. "While we're on the subject, I need someone to compete with me on the quest. Just Charles asked Cheryl Van Snoogle-Something."

"I think Luke said he was asking Kami Rahm," I added.

"What about Dayna?" Sophie asked.

"Ditzy Dayna isn't going to be able to help us," Ben said.

"But she will make it more fun," Sammie said.

"I need to win," I said.

"Who else is there?" Ben asked.

"Dayna is smarter than she looks," Sophie said.

"Her name is Ditzy Dayna. Is she smarter than she acts?" I asked.

LATER THAT DAY, I had to make a bathroom run. I pushed the door of Max Mulvihill's Comfort Station open. Normally, when entering a middle school bathroom, you would expect a stale and foul odiferous punch in the face, but the sweet aroma of freshly-baked chocolate chip cookies danced with my senses. I entered the privately-run bathroom with pure joy.

"Aus the Boss! Or should I say, 'Sir Aus the Boss'?" Max Mulvihill said with a smile. He pulled out a shiny silver pocket watch and flipped it open. "I've been expecting you."

Of course he was. Max had his finger on the pulse of Cherry Avenue Middle School like no other. I had no idea how he knew everything that was going on. "Aus is fine," I said, smiling. I looked around the bright bathroom. There was wood paneling instead of the usual tile and a few leather recliners in the corners.

"Is that pumpkin I smell?" I asked, taking in the glorious scents.

"It is, indeed. I have a pumpkin bread in the oven that's to die for," Max said.

"Sounds wonderful," I said. "Speaking of dying, I've challenged Randy Warblemacher to an epic medieval quest at the upcoming medieval Renaissance fair."

"I heard about that," Max said, thoughtfully. "Tell me what troubles you."

"I'm going to get my butt kicked. I've been training, but I need an edge. I need to be able to handle anything and everything that he could throw at me. Like literally throw at me. He beat me up with a wooden sword and threw me in the garbage pail on our last field trip," I said as I felt my cheeks flush. My facial cheeks. Not my butt cheeks.

Max just looked at me nodding. I needed some comfort after bearing my soul to the school's bathroom attendant, so I grabbed a warm, soft cookie and gobbled it down. One day I would ask him about how the heck he ran a private bathroom service with ovens, chandeliers, and hot tubs inside a public school, but that was not the time.

I wasn't sure how to bring up Ben and how Max had

helped him during Battle of the Bands. I didn't want to get Ben in trouble, but I really needed some help, so I just went for it. "My best friend, Ben Gordon, came to you for some help over the summer. You helped him become one with the drums. I need to be one with my sword. And the pain. Thanks for that, by the way. Free tickets for life for you and a guest any time Mayhem Mad Men play a gig."

"Ahhh, young Benjamin. A good kid. And good student."

"That he is. So, can you help?" I asked, eagerly.

"If I didn't know you better, I'd be insulted by the question." Max held the pocket watch up in front of my face and swung it gently from side to side. "Are you familiar with the topic of symbolic imagery?"

"No," I said, my eyelids getting heavy.

"No matter," Max said, continuing to lull me into a

trance. "Are you familiar with The Thing from Marvel's Fantastic Four comic?"

"Of course," I said, like he was crazy for asking.

"Then you know that not only does he have incredible strength, his body is covered with a flexible, rock-like hide enabling him to survive impacts of great force without sustaining injury."

"Mmm, hmmm," I mumbled, as Max continued to swing the watch in front of me.

"And should you wish to do so, you may transform your body into The Thing, acquiring that same protective covering."

"Does it have to be neon orange?" I mumbled.

"It can be any color you like," Max said, softly.

"You are The Thing," Max whispered.

"I am The Thing," I said, monotone.

I FOUND myself walking down the east wing of my school, not sure where I'd been or where I was going. I looked at my watch and realized that it was the middle of fifth period. I decided to head there and take a peek. I didn't know if I had been there already or what. I felt really weird.

And then I saw Derek heading my way. "Where are you going?" he asked. "You look lost."

"I'm fine," I said, not sure that I was actually fine. I felt spectacular. Strong as an ox. But I had lost time, which was never good. I hoped my beautiful mind wasn't leaving me.

"You ready for the quest? Randy's not who you should be worrying about."

"Why not?"

"Because Sammie and me are entering," Derek said, pleased with himself.

I didn't like the idea of them competing together. Sammie had a crush on my brother from the time she met him up until Randy moved into town last year. I knew it would end badly because my brother was a jerk. "If you're going to compete with Sammie, there's one requirement."

"What's that?" Derek asked, amused.

I didn't know how to say what I wanted to say to Derek without getting pummeled, but I did my best. "You know how people always say to be yourself?"

"Yeah? What about it?"

"Well, don't be." Was that polite enough?

9

I had fully healed from my first training session. Well,
at least physically. There may still have been some
unresolved emotional trauma. But I was determined
to get stronger. The crew had gathered in my backyard
again. I stood in front of Luke and Just Charles in my
modern medieval armor. They stared back at me as if I was
Thanksgiving dinner and they were starving.

Ben looked at me and asked, "Ready to go?"

I took a deep breath and exhaled. "Bring. It. On."

Luke attacked full force with a piercing scream. I
blocked it, matching his force.

I had a strange desire to scream out, "I am The Thing!"

The pain melted away. I absorbed each blow like a tram-
poline with a fat guy on it. I just kept bouncing back. I
blocked some while my ribs and arms took some as well. I
was in the zone. I still stunk with the sword, but something
felt different. I felt stronger. Invincible, even.

Luke connected with a crushing blow to my ribs, which
would've normally killed me. Luke usually didn't know

when to stop, but even he knew he connected pretty well. He stopped and looked at me quizzically.

"Are you okay?" Just Charles asked.

I laughed. They all looked at me like I was crazy. "No, I'm not." I gritted my teeth. "Hit. Me. Harder."

Ben jumped in between us and said, "Okay, that's enough of this for now. I think we may have disconnected his brain from the rest of his body or something. Let's move on."

I threw down my stick and catcher's mask angrily. "Man up! We're never going to beat Randy when you swing like a bunch of nerds!"

"Chill, dude. That's all we got," Luke said. "Have you gone insane?"

"My mind has never been clearer." I looked at Ben and said, "What's next?"

Ben walked me over to a big tree toward the back of our property. It had a thick branch that jutted out over us with a tire swing hanging from it. Only it had been modified. There were four targets in a circle secured around the rope above the tire, about chest height.

"What the heck is this?" I asked. "Did you build this?"

"Yes. I was out here at six this morning." Ben stepped up to the targets and smacked one with his hand. It spun around in a circle like a ceiling fan, but with the blades vertical instead of horizontal. "As you can see, I've done some preparation this time. This is a jousting target. You're going to need that equipment and a bike," he said, nodding to my catcher's gear and hockey stick.

"Okay," I said, nervously. "What the heck do we need a bike for?" I asked.

"We don't, if you have a horse." Ben asked.

"Fair point," I said.

I grabbed my bike from the shed and rolled it back over to the crew. It took me a few tries, but I finally got my heavily armored leg over the seat. I was a powerful knight already. I hopped up onto the bike and steadied myself. Ben handed me a hockey stick.

"Your lance, my Liege," Ben said with an English accent. He backed away and continued, "The object is to hit the target with your lance without the target swinging around and smacking you in the head." Ben tapped the target above him. It spun around quickly again. "It will teach you to attack and defend at the same time."

"Are we going to ride horses and joust at the quest?" Just Charles asked, surprised.

"Dr. Dinkledorf won't say. I bugged his desk, but even that has come up empty. Although it did confirm that he snores loudly and says, 'Alas' too often."

"I admire your commitment to my quest," I said, with a humble nod.

"It is my pleasure, my lord," Ben said, taking a bow. "Attacketh when ready."

I nodded and walked back the bike about fifty feet. I wanted to hit the target with some speed so I could blast right through without the target whacking me in the back of the head.

I stared at the target as Ben, Just Charles, and Luke watched me from off to the side about ten feet in front of our pool. I took a deep breath, pulled down the catcher's mask, gripped the hockey stick in the middle, and tucked the blade under my armpit. I lined the grip of the stick up at the target.

I let out a blood-curdling scream as I peddled across the grass. It was harder than I thought it would be. The grass was a bit bumpier than the blacktop and I could only steer with one hand, as my other aimed the lance at the target. I peddled as fast as I could until I was only about ten feet away. I was going at a decent rate of speed. With only a few feet left, I stopped peddling so I could focus on the target.

I steadied the tip of my lance a few feet out in front of my noble BMX steed. My lance connected with the target with a thwack. I cheered as I rode past the target. It was a short-lived celebration as the target spun around with lightning speed, connecting with the back of my head. The force of the blow pushed my body forward. My horse wobbled out of balance as my eyes attempted to refocus. I looked up to see Ben, Just Charles, and Luke diving in all directions to avoid being trampled by my stallion.

My body fought gravity at every turn. I regained control of my horse as it slowed down, but failed to see the stones surrounding the pool. My horse's front tire connected with the stone with a pop and stopped abruptly. My horse whinnied and kicked its hind legs. The force and trajectory of it tossed me from the saddle. I soared over the stones and into the shallow end of the pool with a splash. Bubbles rushed around me as I sunk to the bottom of the pool, the weight of the equipment dragging me down.

I stood up in the shallow end of the pool, fully equipped and sopping wet, to find my crew at the edge of the pool, staring at me, on the verge of laughter.

"Care for a refreshing dip in the pool?" I asked. "Did they have in-ground pools in medieval times?"

They all burst out laughing.

"Thank you for your support," I said with a smirk. I took off the mask and tossed it at Luke's feet, who was laughing especially hard.

The crew helped me out of the pool.

Ben said. "I think we're done for the day."

As I took off my soaking-wet equipment, I said, "There's still one thing we need to figure out." I looked at Ben, "Did you ask anyone yet?"

"Yeah, I asked Ditzy Dayna," he said.

"Ahhh, farts, dude," I said. I didn't have anything against Ditzy Dayna per se, but she wasn't exactly medieval quest material. Not that the rest of us were, either.

"Sorry. I don't know any other girls. Well, none that would actually accept."

"Okay," I said, exhaling.

"She thought I was a cute new student," Ben said, smiling. "I didn't tell her we've known each other since kindergarten." He looked at me seriously. "Don't worry. I can help you. She won't even know what's going on."

"Yeah, me too," Just Charles said. "Cheryl wants to win, though, so I've gotta keep helping you on the down low."

"I want to win," Luke said. "Kami said I was cute. I need to win for her honor."

"She has terrible eyesight," I said.

"Funny," Luke said, smirking.

"We have to pick up the costumes tomorrow, right?" Ben asked.

"Oh, yeah. Forgot about that. We're gonna look awesome in tunics," I said, unhappily.

AFTER SCHOOL, all of the participants from Cherry Avenue gathered to pick up costumes outside the gym, with the opportunity to try them on in the locker rooms. I didn't want to wear the tunic any longer than I had to, so I didn't bother trying it on.

I stood next to Sophie, Ben, Luke, and Just Charles in front of Dr. Dinkledorf, my life in his hands.

"You said there was a tunic, which is bad enough, but nobody said anything about tights," I said, my shoulders slumping.

I heard bells jingling and then Mr. Muscalini's voice behind me say, "If I can wear 'em, so can you."

I turned around to see Mr. Muscalini in red tights with a red, black, and white jester costume on and a matching hat. Both the tips of his hat and his curled shoes had bells on them, as did the cuffs around his sleeves.

"Uhh, you're looking spectacular, sir," I said, not sure why I said it, because that was not at all the case.

Mr. Muscalini said, "Dinkledorf, I thought we talked about going sleeveless?"

"Alas, on such short notice and with a strict budget, custom outfitting was just not possible."

Mr. Muscalini shook his head, frustrated. "You're ruining my whole life's philosophy."

Dr. Dinkledorf looked pleasantly surprised. "What's your philosophy? I love a good philosophical discussion."

"Sun's out, guns out," Mr. Muscalini whined.

"There were no guns in the Middle Ages, I'm afraid."

Mr. Muscalini turned with a huff and jingled away, body hunched over in despair.

Dr. Dinkledorf looked at me while shaking his head. "How is training going?" he whispered. "Do you think you can win?"

"It's going okay. I'm going to try. I'll do my best."

I turned around to Mr. Muscalini's booming voice, "Your best? We don't give our best around here!"

"We don't?" I asked, confused.

"Winners don't try!"

"They don't?" Ben asked.

"Winners win, Davenport! Find the will! Find the way! In the immortal words of the master Jedi Yoda, 'Do or do not! There is no try!'"

I nodded, energy surging through my body. He just threw down a Star Wars quote on me. It was not something to take lightly.

"Any advice on how I can win?" I asked, excited.

Mr. Muscalini shrugged. "Don't wear tights. These things are stifling."

"Thanks," I said. "That will certainly help me slay the dragon."

Dr. Dinkledorf chuckled. "Alas, I can't give away any specific hints. The Quest Master has sworn me to secrecy. But I will tell you this. It will take brains, strength, courage, and teamwork to win the crown." he said with an English accent.

Mr. Muscalini looked impressed. He said, "That was pretty good. You should talk that way all the time. I've often wondered if my teaching would be more effective with a Scottish accent."

"Really?" I asked. We were all a little bit dumbfounded. Or a lot. I looked at my crew.

Mr. Muscalini looked at me like I was an idiot. "Sometimes, I wonder about you, Davenport." He turned and left, jingling all the way.

BEN and I sat on the bean bag chairs in my room, strategizing after school.

"How bad do you think I'm gonna lose?" I asked.

"I don't know. You kinda went psycho against Luke and Just Charles. You may be okay," Ben said. "But it's hard to tell against other nerds. I can't train you good enough when all we have are Luke and Just Charles as your opponents."

"I know. We need to amp up my training." I stared up at the ceiling. "I think I have an idea."

"What's that?"

"Derek."

AFTER DEREK GOT HOME from football practice, I walked into my den to find him on the couch and said, "Derek, I need your help."

"No."

"It involves beating me up."

"I'm in."

"With a little training sprinkled in."

"We'll see about that," Derek said. "Let's start with the beatings," he said with a smile. I had never seen him happier. See what I had to deal with?

Derek stood up and walked over to me. He looked down at me. "Do you want me to just punch you in the face a few times?"

"Yeah, that's not what we had in mind," Ben said, tentatively.

"Alright, stomach then. It's best if you don't clench and you just let me blast you."

"Hold on a sec," I said. "I'm not training to fight Rocky. I have to become a knight."

"Oh, right. Why don't we do some pull-ups then?"

"Can't do any," I said, sheepishly.

"Push-ups?"

"Not my thing."

"Okay. I have an idea. Suit up in my goalie equipment. I'll take slap shots at you."

Ben nodded. "I like that idea. It'll toughen you up and improve your reflexes."

"Okay," I said, reluctantly.

We went out to the garage and I suited up in Derek's old hockey goalie equipment. There were two ginormous leg pads, a chest protector, and the same gloves and helmet that I used last time.

Derek grabbed a stick and a few balls. I waddled out to the driveway and then strapped on my helmet.

"Try not to get hit," Derek said.

Without warning, he fired shot after shot at me.

"Hey!" I yelled. And then an "Ahh, farts!"

The balls either bounced off me or the garage door behind me and rolled right back to him, so there were no breaks. It was like dodge ball, except rapid fire. Derek was like a machine, crushing balls at me at warp speed. I ducked. I dodged. I danced. I spun. I took a direct shot to my left butt cheek, which ended up doubling in size. I sat lopsided for about a week after that, always looking like I was about to tip over. It wasn't fun. Everybody in school thought I was trying to squeak out a fart or something.

Anyway, back to Derek. He blasted me as hard or harder than Randy ever could, which was good. But then I realized I needed more offense. I was ready to take a beating, but I didn't have any skill to actually beat Randy.

"Okay," I said, gasping for air. I tore off the mask and threw it on the grass.

"That was awesome!" Derek said. "Any time you want to do that, I'm in."

"The quest is in like two days, so I'm pretty certain I won't ever be doing that again. But..."

"But what?" Derek asked.

"I still need to learn how to fight with a sword."

"I'll beat you up with a sword! This is one of the best days of my life," Derek said.

"I don't need you to beat me up. I need to learn how to beat you. And Randy."

"Well, you can't beat me, but Randy's easy. He can't go left."

"That's what Dad always says about you."

"Yeah, but he's worse. Once I played against him enough in basketball, I realized that he only dribbled with his left just to fake left. He crossed right back over to the other side."

"I don't know how that helps."

"I don't know, either. Chop off his right hand," Derek said with a shrug.

"I'm pretty sure there won't be any chopping," I said. "I don't even know if there will be any sword fighting. I wish I knew what was going to be on the quest."

The front door opened and my dad walked outside and down the stairs. He looked over at us, surprised.

"Are you guys actually playing something together?"

"Yeah, we're prepping for the quest," I said. "You have any sword fighting experience?" I asked, hopefully.

"No, but I took karate. I could probably teach you a thing or two. And then Google the rest."

Ben said, "Great idea! I'll find some drills while you do that." Ben was on his phone in a second, thumbing away.

My dad thought for a moment. "Think of fighting like math."

"Huh?" we all said, looking at each other.

"It's all about circles and angles," he said, simply.

I frowned, thinking. "How so?"

My dad stepped forward. He held his fist straight out and rotated in a full circle.

"That's one of the best dance moves I've ever seen you do," I said to him.

"Very funny. That wasn't a dance move. My moves are epic."

Derek and I looked at each other and laughed.

"Moving on," my dad said. "I just made a circle around my body. That's my defensive circle. It is my mission to keep you out of my circle, so you can't hurt me. Now, your circle might be a little bigger, because with a sword, the attacker's reach is longer, right? Understand?"

"I think so," I said. "But how do I keep Randy out of my circle?"

"You have to move and change angles."

"If I come at you," my father said while walking toward me, "and you walk back, I have you at an advantage. But, if you change angles, you can counter strike. Don't let him into your circle, step to the side, and then step into his circle from that new angle and attack."

"What if he gets into my circle?" I asked.

"Don't let him in. But if he gets in, block it and change angles. If you stand in front of Randy and trade blows, he's going to win. He's bigger, faster, and stronger. Those are the facts. So, you need to fight smarter, which you are. Got it?"

"Yep. Keep him out of my circle and change the angles on him. Simple math. With swords. This should be fun," I said, smirking.

"All right," my dad said. "Derek has practice, so we'll work more after if you want."

"Okay. Thanks, Dad," I said and then looked at Derek and said, "Thanks for your help, too."

"No problem. I've always enjoyed kicking your butt."

My dad shook his head, chuckling as they walked away.

Ben looked up from his phone and said, "I am now master of the sword. Well, I at least found something good that I think will help."

"What?"

"Bubbles," Ben said with a serious look on his face.

"Bubbles? What are you talking about?"

"Do you still have that bubble machine we used to play with a few years ago?"

"I think so. I think it's in one of those cabinets," I said, still curious. "Bubbles?"

"Bubbles are the way," Ben said. "I'll get the bubble machine. You take off those pads."

"Okay, boss," I said. "Bubbles? Are you sure?"

"I've never been so sure of anything in my life," Ben said, heading into the garage.

I stared at him as he walked away. "Bubbles," I said to myself.

Ben was back with the bubble machine by the time I got all of my pads off. He put it down on the ground and stood up.

"Bubbles," he said.

"Just tell me what I'm supposed to do," I said.

"Okay. Next, we'll work on your impatience, young Jedi."

I ignored him.

"Think of the bubbles as Randy's weaknesses, openings in his defense that you want to strike. They could be anywhere. You have to wait for them to get to you and pop them with the butt of the hockey stick."

I laughed. "You said, 'Butt.'"

"And you want to become a knight? Do you think Randy is making butt jokes?"

"Randy's never made a butt joke in his life. And the world is a better place for it," I said.

"True," Ben said. He flipped the switch on the bubble machine and yelled, "En garde!"

The machine whirred and then started churning out bubble after bubble. I jutted the stick handle out toward them, popping them one by one. I sliced and whacked every bubble that came my way.

"Don't let any hit the ground!" Ben yelled.

I looked down and there were about a dozen bubbles floating at knee height. I quickly dropped to one knee and sliced horizontally across them, popping more than half and finished the rest as I brought my sword back across. I smiled, but it was short lived as the bubbles kept coming.

I stabbed and sliced until my arms felt like they would fall off, striking every one of Randy's weaknesses like I was the Man in Black from The Princess Bride. I reminded myself to watch it again before the quest for more inspiration. It had the best movie sword fight in history.

My heart was pumping so fast, I thought it might pop like a bubble, but I kept pushing. There were only a few more bubbles left. I sliced across my body with both hands, pulverizing the final two bubbles. I threw down my sword and thrust my fists into the air.

"Victory!" I yelled.

I looked over at Ben, who stared back at me with no emotion.

"I just slayed the dragon, dude. What's wrong?"

"The machine was only on low. There are two higher settings."

"No!" I yelled, falling to my knees. I held my head in my hands as I questioned if I would ever succeed in becoming a knight. "Bubbles," I cried. I slumped to the ground. I lay on my side, staring at the hateful bubbles still floating out like a factory assembly line.

"Again," Ben said.

"I just want some grilled cheese and lemonade," I groaned. "And my mommy's love."

"Knights don't drink lemonade! Get up, you lazy lout! Randy is a champion. He's going to cut you to ribbons if this is all you have!"

I pounded the ground with both hands and let out a scream from the bottom of my soul. I stood up after my hands stopped hurting, growling at the universe, while Ben flipped the bubble machine up to the highest setting. The bubbles flew out of the machine like somebody farted. Badly.

"I can't do it," I said.

"You can and you will. Now pop those bubbles, Sir Austin!"

I closed my eyes, took a deep breath, and decided to take it one bubble at a time. Focused and ready, I opened my eyes to a sea of bubbles. I could barely see Ben through them all. I gripped the hockey stick and pretended that each bubble was Randy's stupid face.

I jabbed, poked, head-butted, karate-kicked, and sliced every bubble that came my way. The bubbles were dwindling. I sliced across my body with both hands, chopping at least twenty bubbles in half. The momentum took me around in a circle, but I kept at it. I rotated around and sliced the remaining bubbles with two slices in an 'X' strike. With nothing left but the machine, I spun once more, lifted the stick above my head with both hands and sliced down on top of the machine.

The bubble machine cracked with a pop and bounced up into the air. It tumbled over and crashed onto its side, its gooey, soapy brains spilling out into the driveway.

I looked at Ben with fire in my eyes. "I am Sir Austin Davenport and I am not a Knight!!"

"What?" Ben asked, confused.

"I am *the* knight! Fear me like you fear your worst nightmare when the Dark Knight cometh for you!"

"I think I just peed a little in my pants," Ben said, sheepishly. "That was really scary."

"I'm ready for the quest! Well, after I take a bubble bath."

10

I relaxed in a soothing bubble bath for what seemed like hours. I no longer hated the bubbles nor did I want to pop them. In fact, I even made a few bubbles of my own, if you know what I mean, as I lay there in the warm water.

Once I was done with the bath, I drained the tub, dried off, and wrapped a towel around my waist. I walked down the hallway past Derek's room and into mine. Derek was talking on the phone.

"Dude, it's gonna be bad. Randy's gonna crush him. It might not be as bad as the garbage pail, but he can't hang with Randy. I know. I don't know what he was thinking, dude."

I tried to ignore him as I continued on to my room, but his words continued to echo in my mind. "He can't hang with Randy."

I got dressed and then just chilled for a while in my room before dinner. The confidence I had after popping all of those bubbles seemed to disappear when my mind shifted to actually beating a real person. I was kidding myself if I thought I could beat Randy.

Did I make a terrible mistake? Did one impulsive moment ruin my life? In what world did I think I could beat Randy Warblemacher, athlete extraordinaire, at anything physical? Especially when he was a cheater on top of it all. And there was no backing out. I had dropped the gauntlet over the Speaker of Doom. The whole school heard me challenge Randy.

After a heavy white-boarding strategy session, I determined that my best option was to transfer to a different school, but that would mean leaving behind my friends and Sophie, which was not an option, so I was back at square one: getting my butt kicked in front of the whole medieval town of Chester.

~

MY FAMILY GATHERED FOR DINNER. It was the whole crew,

which didn't happen that often with Leighton in high school and all of Derek's sporting commitments. I sat quietly at the table, thoughts of angst bouncing around my head.

My mom asked me, "How was training?"

"Not bad," I said, staring at my food as I ate.

My dad followed with another question. "In a totally unconnected issue, have you noticed that we need new garbage pail lids?"

"Sorry, they make good shields."

My dad looked at me and said, "You okay? What's going on in that big 'ole brain of yours?"

"Nothing good," I said, stuffing a piece of a dinner roll in my mouth.

"What do you mean, sweetie?" Mom asked.

"I'm just nervous about the quest. Randy's gonna kick my butt tomorrow."

"Oh, that's tomorrow?" Derek asked.

Idiot. "Yep. Do you remember asking Sammie? She's going to be really disappointed if and when you mess up. I mean, how did you even forget that? You just asked her."

"Yeah, I'm over it. It's kinda boring to me."

"So why did you ask her?" Leighton chimed in. She shook her head. "She's too nice for you."

"Leighton!" my mother yelled.

"It's true, Mom. He's gonna mess this whole thing up. We're gonna have to move. The Howells are gonna hate us. We're gonna have to move to Bear Creek and they don't even have a Starbucks."

"So why did you ask her?" Dad asked Derek.

Derek shrugged. "I don't know. She's a cheerleader. I'm a football player. Isn't that how it's supposed to go?"

"That's not a great reason, son," Dad responded.

"She's the same girl you grew up next to for the last

eleven years," Mom said.

"You're an idiot," I said. "You're still taking her, right?"

Derek shrugged. "I guess so. I'll have to find a way to spice things up. Wearing tights isn't it."

We all chuckled. I still thought he was an idiot and I was afraid that he would crush Sammie's hopes and dreams.

"Speaking of tights. Mom, did you iron my tunic?" I asked.

"Not yet, honey."

"I can't have a wrinkly tunic! It's bad enough that I have to wear an ironed one!"

"Calm down. It'll get done." Dad looked at me and asked, "What else can you do to get ready?"

I shrugged. "I don't know." And then it hit me. "Oh, no! I didn't prepare for the rose ceremony."

I spent the rest of the night and half of the early morning working on ideas on how I would present the rose to Sophie. I wanted to get it right because it was likely to go very wrong from there. I decided to write her a song. And I crushed it. You'll hear it later, don't you worry. It's not Mayhem Mad Men quality, but I was happy.

I woke up the next morning. It was tunic time! I wasn't all that enthused, as I'm sure you've picked up on. My dad drove Derek, Sammie, Sophie, and me to the festival. Of course, Derek sat in the front seat, leaving Sammie alone in the back, which was fine with me. His chivalry was less than inspiring.

My father dropped us off at the entrance to the medieval town of Chester. It was wild and totally different than when we had been there for the field trip. Hundreds of people milled about, most dressed in medieval garb. Men wore tunics, cloaks, and even chainmail, a type of armor with chain links, which looked really cool, but seemingly difficult to pee in. Well, they appeared quite easy to pee in. It was more peeing out of it that looked difficult. They were all heavily armed with swords and maces. Women mostly wore flowing dresses with crowns of jewels or flowers, although some wore more military-like garb with swords. There were even a few knights in shiny armor creaking and squeaking about.

"Wow, this is amazing!" Sophie said. She pointed to the town center where we had been just a few weeks earlier. "I've never been to one of these. Look, there's a juggler, a fortune teller, and look at those turkey legs!"

My eyes widened as they focused upon a vendor selling oversized turkey legs. "I'm totally getting one of those!" I yelled.

"Me, too!"

"Really?" I asked, looking at her curiously.

"A girl can't eat a giant turkey leg?" Sophie asked, annoyed.

"I think you can do anything you set your mind to, my fair lady," I said with an English accent, taking a page out of Dr. Dinkledorf's book, hoping it would keep me from getting beaten up before I even saw Randy.

"Nice save," Sophie said, with a smirk.

We walked around the center of town. There was the stage area with the five stockades, this time filled with people taking pictures. A woman breathed on a stick with dramatic flair. A red flame burst out of nowhere. It was awesome.

"What?" I said, surprised. "That was awesome."

"Ooh, there's a bard!" Sophie said, running ahead.

I followed her up to a man dressed in a green tunic and matching hat. He kind of looked like Robin Hood. He sat up against a stone wall with a small acoustic guitar in his hand. He strummed it as he sang, "They come from the east and the west to partake in the noble quest. Only two will survive to become royals tonight, once they pass the quest master's great test. It will take skill and the will- to win. I hope you have a strong chin. It'll take courage and brains. Cheat and you may find yourself in chains. If you do this in a cinch, you just may be our prince. And my ladies, if you're the best, you could be our new princess. Step up and join our great quest. As long as you sign a waiver for danger and liability, our prince or princess you could be!"

We clapped as the bard finished his song. Ben caught my eye and hurried over with Ditzy Dayna.

"Hey, what's up?" I asked.

Sophie looked at Dayna and asked, "Did you get a haircut?"

"Yeah, I just walked in front of an axe-throwing contest. I didn't even have to pay for it."

Ben shook his head and mouthed, "You were right."

I turned when I heard a man behind me say, "Care for a drink, my Lord?"

I looked down at the sparse cart he was pushing.

"What do you have?" I asked, only seeing one lonely pitcher.

"It's dirty water. Did you think they had soda in medieval times?"

"I'll pass. Thanks."

"So be it, my lord," he said, frustrated and walked away, pushing the cart. "Dirty water here! Get your authentic, medieval water here!"

We continued to look around. Art displays were everywhere. I remembered Dr. Dinkledorf saying that art was an important part of the Renaissance period. They had tons of art for sale and there were even painting portraits of people wearing their medieval garb.

Sophie looked at me and asked, "Do you want to get a painting done of us?"

I shrugged. "Sure."

"How about after we win?"

"Okay," I said.

And then I heard jingling behind me. I turned around with a smile to see Mr. Muscalini heading our way. He was in his full jester costume, although the sleeves were missing, revealing his hulking arms. His face was also painted half white and half red, split right down the middle.

Mr. Muscalini looked at us with a smile and said in a high-pitched voice, "Who assembled the Knights of the Round Table?"

I almost started laughing before he even gave us the

punchline, just based on his outfit, makeup, and voice. I looked at Sophie and shrugged.

"I don't know," she said.

"Why Sir Cumference, of course!" Mr. Muscalini laughed like a wacko, which, of course, he was. He stopped dead in his tracks and then pointed, surprised. "Look! Under there!"

We all turned to look, but saw nothing.

"Under where?" I asked.

"Ha ha! I made you say underwear! Did people actually wear underwear during the Renaissance period?" Mr. Muscalini laughed and bounced off to the next group.

My friends all laughed at me. I shrugged.

I looked at Ben and asked, "Did you hear the bard yet? He's awesome."

"No, you wanna go back before the quest?"

Sophie nodded.

"Sure," I said.

We made our way back to him. The bard was singing a new song to the crowd that had gathered around him.

The bard sang, "One need not be noble at birth. To take the castle and crown, you must be noble in heart and show your worth! Hop on top of your noble steed, but make sure that first you have peed, because you're going on a long journey to becoming royalty."

"But should you stray from chivalraaaaaay, you'll be reduced to an average Joe. To the dungeon you will go! While they'll never tell you straight- rumors swirl of prisoners who have made the great escape!"

"See, I told you this guy was good," I said to Ben.

"Yeah, I mean, Dr. Dinkledorf didn't even warn us to pee first. This is helpful stuff."

"He's awesome. Do you think I can download this from iTunes?" Ditzy Dayna asked.

"Yeah, probably not," Ben said. "But it is catchy." He continued, singing the bard's song, "Hop on top of your noble steed! And don't forget to pee pee!"

"I don't think those were the words."

"Close enough."

After the applause died down, the bard started a new song, "In the deep of the Dragon's Keep, the Knights of the Undead guard the dragon's egg. Should you survive their certain doom, you may find yourself alone in a dragon's bedroom. If you're lucky enough not to wakey wake- the dragon, grab the egg to takey take. And vanish. Or you might find, that you have a burned behind, and that you haven't fled, but joined the Knights of the undead instead..."

Sophie asked, "Do you want to go to the fortune teller?"

"Sure," I said with a shrug.

"We're gonna stay here and catch a few more songs," Ben said.

"Okay. Communicateth later, we will," I said.

Sophie and I turned to leave, but I turned back around quickly when I heard a familiar voice.

"Do you want some authentic medieval water, my lady?" the dirty-water vendor asked Ditzy Dayna, holding a cup in front of her.

"No!" I yelled.

Ditzy Dayna shrugged, grabbed the cup, and threw it back down her throat before we could stop her.

"What's wrong?" Dayna asked.

I looked at Sophie and then back at Dayna. "Umm, nothing."

SOPHIE and I sat at a small, wooden table inside a tattered tent in front of the fortune teller, Lady Tabitha. She eyed us mysteriously. She had piercing blue eyes and a matching jewel on her hat over her forehead.

"I've been expecting you," she said.

Our eyes widened.

"Really?" Sophie asked.

"Yes, it has been foretold," Lady Tabitha said, while moving her hands in a wide arc in dramatic fashion.

Sophie looked at me and whispered, "This is incredible."

"Now, let me see your hands."

Sophie and I both put our hands on the table in front of us. Lady Tabitha inspected them with her eyes and then took Sophie's hand and traced the lines on Sophie's palm with her finger.

"Very interesting," Lady Tabitha said, taking my hand.

"What?" Sophie asked, on the edge of her seat.

"Shushie!" Lady Tabitha said.

I was pretty sure that wasn't a medieval term, but I let it slide.

Lady Tabitha closed her eyes, seemingly falling into a trance. "Betrayal," she said, mysteriously. "Revenge! Such darkness I see." She opened her eyes and looked at us. "This is going in an unexpected and dangerous direction. Are you prepared to continue?"

Sophie and I looked at each other, eyes wide, and nodded.

"Very well. Where was I? Ahh, yes. Revenge! Very dark, indeed. Yet, I also see light. Triumph over evil." Lady Tabitha grabbed my other hand and studied the lines. "Courage in the face of insurmountable odds. A budding romance, oh yes, I see it very clearly. This part...it's a little fuzzy," Lady Tabitha squeezed her eyes shut. "I see it now. True love's kiss." She opened her eyes and looked at us with a raised eyebrow.

I glanced over at Sophie to see her blushing. Was she talking about us? My heart started to pound.

Lady Tabitha snapped her fingers. "Over here, love birds." She continued, "I see a boy."

"What does he do?" Sophie asked, on the edge of her seat.

"He becomes a hero. And a girl becomes a legend!"

Sophie and I looked over at each other with wide grins.

"Now, I see you giving me ten bucks and then leaving," Lady Tabitha said with her hand out.

I reached into my shoe and took out some money. Tunics and tights don't have pockets. It's just one of their many shortcomings. I handed Lady Tabitha the money, with a smile.

Lady Tabitha whispered. "Trust no one. And tell no one what has been prophesized, if that's even a word." She held her hand up. "Wait!" She rubbed her temples with her eyes closed. "Strangely, I also see lots of turkey legs in your future." She opened her eyes and said, "Godspeed on your quest."

As we walked out, Sophie asked with excitement, "Can you believe that?"

"I don't know. Do you think she can really tell the future by looking at our hands. Wouldn't science be able to prove it?" I asked.

Sophie countered, "There are some mystical things that science hasn't been able to prove."

"Like what?" I asked.

A voice whispered in my ear from behind, "Like why she likes you, Peasantfart."

I turned around and looked up at Randy with disgust. "Randolph Nesbitt Warblesucker, we meet again. The circle is now complete," I said in my deepest Darth Vader voice.

"What are you talking about?"

"Ugh. Haven't you ever seen Star Wars? I was quoting Darth Vader." I shook my head. I took a deep breath and regrouped. "It's my fault. You're the evil one, anyway. I shouldn't be quoting Darth Vader. I just wish you could be a better nemesis sometimes."

"I'll try to be better," Randy said.

"Thank you. That's very kind. Now, where were we? Oh, right. I'm going to squash you like a turd," I said.

"Eww, why would you step on a turd? I knew you were weird, Davenfart, but that's just disgusting."

Regan walked up behind Randy and I almost vomited. They were wearing matching tunics. They certainly weren't the ones that Dr. Dinkledorf had given us all. They were red silk or something with shiny, black ropes as belts, and black tights. And worse than that, they each had a golden heart embroidered where their hearts would've been, had they actually had them.

"You know what's even more disgusting? Those matching outfits. Do you have your names on the back?"

"No," Randy said with serious attitude. "I really wanted it, but it wasn't authentic."

"We're going to crush you two," Regan said with a smirk. She held up a turkey leg in front of Randy's face. "Eat up, my baby waby."

Sophie and I looked at each other and nearly puked.

Randy took a tiny bite. Regan took the turkey leg back and took a huge, savage bite herself. Then Regan ran her fingers through Randy's hair, brushing it back, leaving turkey skin and juice in it. Randy tried to keep a smile on his face, but he hated dirt and grossness.

"Don't you just love when I touch your hair?" Regan said.

"Mmm, hmm," Randy said.

I recoiled, waiting for Randy to snap. He wasn't the kind of guy who would accept a turkey rub. He once reprimanded me for offering him a slice of pizza because its oily nature would not be good for his skin. But I was shocked at what he said.

"I love it when you rub greasy turkey leg fat in my hair, Reagy Weagy."

I laughed and then cupped my hands and yelled to anyone who would listen, "Welcome to Barf City! Population two!"

11

Sophie pulled me away from Randy and Regan as they baby-talked to each other. They were so involved with feeding each other turkey leg bites, I think they forgot we were even there, which was fine by me.

We weaved in and out of small packs of people until we were a good distance away from them and Lady Tabitha's. We stopped in front of a shop of medieval artifacts, weapons, and jewelry. There were helmets, knives, and swords with gems, statues of castles, dragons, and unicorns, rings, necklaces, and so much more. They even had a wizard hat with a long, white beard attached to it, like Professor Dumbledore.

I followed Sophie as we browsed the shelves and tables. She stopped in front of a group of silver necklaces and inspected one with a charm of a dragon climbing a castle's tower. The turret had a blue gemstone on top of it. It was pretty sweet.

"Do you like this?" Sophie asked.

"Yeah, it's awesome," I said.

Sophie took it off the rack and held it up to my neck. "I want to buy this for you. The dragon will protect you."

"Thanks, but you don't have to."

"I want to," she said with a smile.

As we paid for the necklace, trumpets blared throughout the town.

The shopkeeper, named Ted (were people really named Ted in the Middle Ages?), smiled and said, "It's time to assemble in the great hall for the quest!"

"Let's go," Sophie said.

"Thanks, Ted," I said. I looked at Sophie and whispered, "I have to go to the bathroom."

She looked at me, like really?

I defended myself. "You heard the bard's song. He said to make sure we peed because we're going on a journey."

I was pretty certain the bard wouldn't have said it if it wasn't important. It *was* going to be a long quest. I didn't want to have to go to the bathroom in the middle of it. But who wanted to go to the bathroom at a medieval Renaissance fair with thousands of people? Not this guy. Not unless Max was running it, which wasn't gonna happen.

As we made our way to the great hall, I saw a sign pointing the way to the portapotties. We weaved in and out of people dressed as kings and queens, knights, jesters, and even two people seemingly in a donkey costume. It was weird.

We arrived at the portapotties and my heart leapt. Standing before me was none other than Max Mulvihill. Next to him was a sign that said, 'Medieval Max's'.

"Max!" I yelled, heading toward him.

"You know him?" Sophie asked.

"Yes. It's a long story," I said.

"Sir Aus the Boss. Greetings on this fine morn. Is this the lovely Lady Sophie?"

"It is," I answered. I looked at Sophie and said, "This is Max."

She held out her hand with a smile and said, "It's nice to meet you."

Max bowed. "It is a pleasure, my lady."

"What are you doing here?" I asked.

Max looked at me and shook his head. "I thought you would know by now, Sir Aus. I am here to offer the finest service in portable peeing and pooping. I call it, 'Medieval Max's: Off With Their Heads'."

Sophie and I laughed.

Max pointed to the first of six portapotties. "The first one is open for your usage."

"Thanks," I said. "Be right out." I didn't want Sophie to think I was going to be doing #2 in there.

I opened the door to the portapotty, revealing a spacious bathroom with full amenities, harp music playing from somewhere unknown, and lit by torches. I couldn't believe it. Max had done it again. He turned a normally disgusting bathroom experience into a medieval palace of pee.

Still, peeing with a tunic and tights wasn't exactly easy, but I imagined it was better than the guy with chain mail. I washed my hands in the sink. I was about to dry them in my tunic when I saw disposable hand towels with a Medieval Max logo. There was an axe and a smiling head. It wasn't the best logo in the world, but still.

I exited the medieval bathroom and rejoined Sophie. I looked at Max and said, "That was incredible. How's business going?"

Max's face dropped. "Not great, Sir Aus. That's *the thing*," he said, with a wry smile. "They only sell dirty water here. Nobody's hydrating."

"It's a travesty," I agreed.

"Yeah. Well, a few people have puked, but that's not very helpful for me. *The thing* is, it costs me too much in labor to be cleaning up all that mess."

"I understand," I said. Despite feeling bad about Max's troubles, I felt an odd surge of strength and energy.

"We'd better go," Sophie said to me, and then to Max, "It was a pleasure meeting you."

Max bowed again. "The pleasure was all mine, my lady."

WE GATHERED in the great hall. It was a giant barn with dozens of tables, benches, and a stage with a long table and chairs, and a second smaller table for two with thrones for chairs. There were lit torches flickering in the breeze. Dozens of people were already there, waiting for the Protectors of the Realm and for the great quest to begin.

I had regrouped with my clan of Ben, Ditzy Dayna, Just Charles, Cheryl Van Snoogle-Something, Luke, and Kami Rahm. Sammie was across the way with Derek and Jayden. Randy and Regan were nearby as well.

Luke looked up at the thrones and said, "I gotta get me one of those."

Luke has always had a flair for the dramatic. Over the summer, when our band, Mayhem Mad Men, was really popular, he bought a fur coat for each day of the week. With matching fur underwear. I think he only had one pair of those, though. It probably would've been better if he had one fur coat and seven pairs of underwear, but who am I to judge the fashion choices of others? I was wearing tights.

Kami Rahm asked Sophie, "What did you guys do so far?"

"We went shopping, heard the bard sing, and went to the fortune teller," Sophie answered.

"We saw the fortune teller, too," Kami said, excited.

"What did she tell you?"

Luke butted in, "She said I would win."

Kami corrected him, "She said a boy would become a hero."

"She said that to us, too," Sophie said, disappointed. "I thought she was talking about Austin."

"Maybe she was," I said, not wanting Sophie to be disappointed.

"And a girl would become a legend," Luke said.

"Like we don't already know that," Cheryl Van Snoogle-Something said. "She was talking about the quest."

"She also said there would be betrayal and revenge," I added.

"What a waste of ten bucks," Luke said. "This whole thing is gonna be a bust."

Then the doors burst open. Six guards wearing chain-mail walked in with spears in their hands and swords hanging from their waists. They escorted two men carrying long trumpets and some sort of official-looking dude, who wore a fancy purple tunic with gold trim, who carried a rolled-up piece of paper.

"This is gonna be totally awesome!" Luke yelled.

The guards stopped in front of the crowd and turned to face us. They then marched off in their own directions, spreading out to guard the room, leaving the official-looking dude standing in the center, staring at us with the trumpeters next to him.

The trumpeters raised their instruments and blasted them with a royal-sounding song.

The official-looking dude unrolled the paper. It was so long that it hit the floor. He cleared his throat and then read from the scroll, "Welcome, peasants!"

The crowd mumbled. I looked at Sophie, who shrugged.

The announcer continued, "I ask you to give a warm medieval greeting to the Protectors of the Realm!"

The crowd around us yelled "Huzzah!", as four men and two women entered, wearing similar medieval garb to the guards, only it was shinier and they all had capes.

"I want a cape," I said, as I watched the Protectors enter.

Dr. Dinkledorf led the way with Zorch, Mr. Gifford, and two women that I didn't know behind them. There was also a man at the end of the procession that I couldn't see.

I cheered for them as they entered. And then I froze. The blood drained from body. The face of the man at the end of the procession was clearly in my view and he stared back at me with laser beams. It was Principal Buthaire! But how? And more important, why?

My crew all looked at each other, horrified.

The announcer yelled, "I give you Sir Mason Dinkledorf, Lord of Chester! He pointed to Zorch and said, "Sir Frederick the Flatulant!"

Zorch looked at me and shrugged. I was still in shock at seeing Principal Buthaire.

The announcer continued, announcing Mr. Gifford as, "Sir Geoffrey the Gregarious," and then the two women as, "Lady Dionisia the Deadly" and "Mazelina the Meh!" Mazelina shrugged.

Principal Buthaire and I continued to stare at each other. His hatred of me was written all over his face.

The announcer said, "And Sir Simon the Serious!"

Some people cheered, while many of the students booed. I was too much in shock to join in. As Sir Simon the Serious stopped in front of his seat at the table, he looked at me and smiled.

12

The Protectors remained standing in front of their chairs, staring out to the crowd. Nobody was sure what was supposed to happen next. And then we heard a horse whinnie from afar. The entire crowd looked toward the entrance. The trumpeters blasted their horns again. Thaddeus sat atop a gargantuan horse, both of them adorned in silver armor.

The announcer yelled out, "Sir Thaddeus Dinkledorf, Lord of the Dragons!"

Sir Thaddeus drew his sword and thrust it above his head. He yelled, "Play the trumpets again!" His voice echoed throughout the great hall. Sir Thaddeus pulled back on the reins. The horse kicked its front legs into the air and whinnied again and then sprinted into the great hall, nearly trampling the trumpeters.

Sir Thaddeus pulled back on the reins, stopping the great horse in the center of the hall before us. He sheathed his sword and hopped off the horse with a clank as he hit the ground. Sir Thaddeus nodded to the Protectors, who then seated themselves at the long table on the stage, and turned to the rest of us.

"Hear ye, hear ye. I welcome all of ye! For twenty-five years, you have come near and far to celebrate with us. In honor of this tradition, we shall entertain, nay, entrance you, as you witness the rise of royalty!" Sir Thaddeus paced around the great hall, creaking as he went.

He stopped right in front of us and continued, "Today, anyone who chooses, under thirteen years old, and with a hearty legal waiver signed by a parent or guardian, can conquer the quest and become royalty!"

The crowd cheered with another, "Huzzah!"

Sir Thaddeus turned back to the Protectors and pointed to Dr. Dinkledorf. "Let us pay homage to those that came before us!"

"Huzzah!"

"Two commoners will rise above the rest, and be crowned Prince and Princess of The Realm! Each couple will receive a crown. In order to stand before the Protectors of The Realm for royal consideration, you must overcome challenges, and in return you will be rewarded with jewels to adorn your crown. The more difficult the challenge, the greater the reward! Once your crown is fully bejeweled, you must present yourself before the Protectors of The Realm for judgement."

We all yelled, "Huzzah!" It was fun yelling it.

Sir Thaddeus continued, "You will joust. You will solve unsolvable puzzles. Or perhaps, not. You will send arrows soaring through the air. Secure twelve jewels and you just might find yourself at the Royal table!" He pointed to the thrones and the empty table of two.

Everyone yelled, "Huzzah!"

"That sounds easy enough," someone called out, sarcastically.

Sir Thaddeus raised his hand to quiet the crowd. "There is another way."

The crowd exhaled as Sir Thaddeus continued, "But no man, woman, or child has ever accomplished the feat."

The crowd groaned. The only person smiling in the room was Principal Buthaire.

"Certain tasks are harder than others. You may choose which ones to do. If you find yourself behind your competitors, you may desire to adjust your strategy to attack harder tasks. Perhaps..." Sir Thaddeus drew his sword, thrust it into the air and yelled, "The Dragon's Keep!"

"Huzzah!"

Sir Thaddeus stroked his horse and then walked back toward us, a grave look on his face. "Many have entered the Dragon's Keep, but not all have returned, and none with a dragon's egg!"

Chatter spread throughout the crowd. I looked at Sophie, my eyes bulging. "Let's not do that one!"

"I agree," Sophie said. "That sounds scary."

Ben whispered to me, "The bard sang about that. Something about Knights of the Undead. There's no way I'm going in there."

Sir Thaddeus continued, "Should you break the rules, you might find yourself in a medieval prison. Escape and you can regain the quest. Escape not and you may rot!"

Surprisingly, a few people still yelled, "Huzzah!" at that.

"Now, we begin the presentation of the rose ceremony."

Gulp.

13

I looked around the great hall. There were a lot of pale faces. Even some of the girls looked nervous and all they had to do was grab a rose. I actually had to sing a song that I wrote, and I regretted it big time. But I remembered what Dr. Dinkledorf, I mean, Lord Dinkledorf told me. Sophie would appreciate my putting some thought into the presentation. Most of the other dudes would just hand their partners the rose as quickly as possible, hoping everybody in the whole place had blinked at that exact moment.

We lined up in front of our soon-to-be officially-recognized partners. There were at least twenty groups, maybe more. Sophie and I were right in the middle, surrounded by my crew and the evils, Randy and Regan. It was going to be difficult to win it all. Not only did I have to beat Randy, but a ton of other groups as well.

I smiled weakly at Sophie.

She looked at me with concern. "You didn't plan anything crazy, right?"

"No, it's pretty low key," I lied. "I only wrote a song just for you that I'm going to sing in front of hundreds of people."

"What?" Sophie yelled. She looked around to see everyone nearby staring at her.

Sir Thaddeus called out to the first kid in line, "Sir Jonathan, you may begin."

It went as expected. Most of the kids handed over the rose to their partners without even making eye contact. The first ten were like that. Based on Sophie's response, I was about to just chuck the rose at Sophie and be done with it, but I wanted her to feel special. That's why I wrote it in the first place. And then Randy went. Or should I say, performed?

"Sir Randy, when ready."

Randy stepped forward toward Regan, his eyes staring into hers. He looked over his shoulder at the trumpeters and yelled, "Hit it!"

The trumpeters blasted an intro as Randy started dancing. I wouldn't say it was medieval dancing, because I had no idea how they danced in medieval times, but it wasn't modern, either. It involved pretending to ride a horse. There was some sword play without an actual sword and then singing.

"Regan, my sweet vegan. Will you join me as I stand here flossin'?"

I leaned over and whispered to Sophie, "She's not a vegan! This whole thing is a fraud. She was eating turkey legs!"

Randy continued, "There's nothing more that I want than to be with you and crush Austin. Give me your heart and we can ruin Davenfart! For it is he that I doth detest. Please, be my princess!" Randy carried the final note until the entire place burst into applause.

Randy looked over at me with a menacing look and said, "You're going down, Davenfart."

He didn't scare me. I pointed right back. "It's Sir Davenfart to you, peasant boy!"

I was livid. He never missed an opportunity to bash me. I mean, I bashed him in mine, too, but still. I stared him down as he waved to the crowd, glowing in the applause.

Derek handed his rose to Sammie before Sir Thaddeus even announced him.

Sammie clutched her heart and said, "Isn't he so romantic?"

Ben and Luke made quick presentations to Ditzy Dayna and Kami, so I was up next.

"When ready, Sir Austin," Sir Thaddeus said, his voice bellowing throughout the great hall.

I stepped back, took a deep breath in, attempting to refocus, and cleared my throat. I opened my eyes and stared at Sophie. I tried to block out the hundreds of other eyes staring at me and just focus on the two beautiful ones in front of me. I eased up on the grip around the rose stem as I feared I might choke the poor thing to death.

And then I began my song. I sang, "Are you lookin' for Mr. Knight?" I took a page out of Randy's book and pretended to ride a horse. It was not the best decision. A few pockets of laughter broke out. I continued on. "For my princess, I will fight. We're gonna crush Randayheyhey and his stupid girlfriend, too. And then you and I can rule."

Sophie was shaking her head, half laughing, half embarrassed.

I continued, "If you're looking for Mr. Knight, no need to adjust your sight. Just look right here, I'm the one you revere. I'm your prince, don't you know? Please, do me this honor and accept this rose."

I climbed up on the railing in front of the first row of seats. I held it with one hand while leaning out over the ground and finished the song. "Do you wanna join my quest to prove that we're the best?"

I continued hanging from the railing while holding the rose and singing my final note. Everything was going great until the railing cracked, broke apart, and sent me falling flat on my face. On a positive note, I continued singing all the way down. My music teacher, Mrs. Funderbunk would've been proud. Nobody else was.

I coughed and wiped the dirt out of my eyes. It was so quiet, the place could've been empty except for the two of us. Unfortunately, that was not the case.

Sophie bent down and yelled, "Are you okay?"

"Lovely," I groaned. "My spirit is broken, but that will heal in the afterlife," I mumbled.

I stood up to silence. And then Randy started a slow, patronizing clap. It echoed throughout the great hall.

I reached my hand out to Sophie, holding the crushed red rose out to her. She curtsied and accepted it with a sheepish smile.

"Was that low key enough for you?" I asked.

Sophie shook her head and chuckled.

Thankfully, Just Charles took the pressure off of me.

"That was...interesting," Sir Thaddeus said. "Sir Charles, you may present when ready. And please keep it...simple."

Just Charles did just that. He looked around at the entire great hall staring at him. The rose in his hand began to shake. And then his eyes rolled back in his head and he fell back landing with a thump and a puff of dirt.

Well, I guess passing out wasn't really simple. They had to call the paramedics to check him out, but he was deemed healthy enough to continue on the quest.

We regrouped and stood side by side with our partners, facing the Protectors of The Realm.

Principal Buthaire, er Sir Simon the Serious, stared at me with a smirk. I didn't like the look. It made me feel like he was up to something. I didn't need the quest to be any harder than it was supposed to be.

Sir Thaddeus climbed atop his horse with some difficulty and turned toward us. The horse and I stared at each other.

Sir Thaddeus said, "All step forward who wish to enter the quest!" He pointed to a kid I didn't know. "You, sir. Sir Damon, is it? Did you submit your waiver?"

"Yes, I emailed it last night," he said, softly.

"Are you sure? We don't seem to have it on file. And what about you, Lady Jessica?"

"My mom emailed it this morning," she said, squeakily.

"Well done. We're likely going to need those. As I was saying, only one will rise...well, two, actually. It's a team effort."

The Protectors stood in a line in front of all of the participants, each holding a crown. The announcer stood by a small cart filled with more. The Protectors all stepped forward to the duo immediately in front of them and handed them their crowns.

The Protectors shifted down to the next group of participants. As they walked, I counted quickly, hoping Principal Buthaire would not be the one handing Sophie and me our crown. It would probably be loaded with explosives. I exhaled as I calculated that Dr. Dinkledorf would present to us.

As Lord Dinkledorf received a new crown from the announcer, Principal Buthaire stepped around behind him and said something to him that I couldn't hear. Lord Dinkledorf scooted over, leaving Principal Buthaire lined up with me! And I didn't have a bomb diffusing kit in my tunic. You can't blame me. I told you that they don't have pockets.

Sir Thaddeus called out, "Present the crowns!"

Principal Buthaire walked up to us with a wry smile on his face, holding the crown out to me.

"Good luck!" he said, too loud and excited than anyone should be, particularly him. He leaned in and was more himself, "If you think I'm going to let you win, you haven't learned anything in the past year." He straightened up, rejiggered his chainmail, and waved. "Fare thee well."

14

W e stood in front of the Protectors with our crown and a map that showed the location of each challenge and how many jewels would be awarded when each was conquered. Sir Thaddeus paced around the great hall on his horse.

"There's no sharing or selling of jewels. Each station will record your victory and your points will be tallied upon your presentation," Sir Thaddeus said.

I looked over at Randy. He looked disappointed. I stifled a chuckle, knowing his chief plan was to cheat.

Once again, Sir Thaddeus unsheathed his sword and thrust it above his head. "Are thee ready?"

"Huzzah!"

Mr. Muscalini walked over to a giant gong that stood behind the Protectors' table and smashed it with a gargantuan wooden sledge hammer. It clanked and reverberated throughout the great hall. My ear drums rang.

Kids ran in every direction. I wasn't sure where they were going because none of them had looked at the map.

Sophie quickly unrolled our map. We both scanned it to figure out where to go first.

"Archery gives four jewels. Jousting gives three, unsolvable puzzles three, village pillaging two, castle sieging two, and the dragon's egg twelve," Sophie said.

I pointed to archery and said, "Let's start at the archery and work our way back."

Ben came up beside us with Ditzy Dayna. "We're coming with you."

"Saddle up, partner. We're going to archery," Sophie said and then took off running.

Man, she was fast. Or maybe running in tights somehow restricted blood flow to my legs. I took off right behind her with Ben and Dayna joining in as well. We left the great hall in chaos. Hundreds of people roamed about as quest kids zoomed out of the hall into heavy traffic, not caring about anything but getting jewels.

I followed Sophie to the outer ring of the town center, which was less crowded, and hustled our way through the thinner traffic. As we approached the archery challenge, I gasped to catch my breath. Unfortunately, none of us had the foresight to add cardio to my knight training routine. And Randy and Regan were already at an archery station, testing out their bow.

There was only one target left open by the time we got our bow and arrows from the station supervisor and it just happened to be right next to my old pal, Randy. I was ecstatic to have Randy watch me try to hit a target. We hadn't trained for that, either. I reminded myself to fire Ben as soon as we finished.

"Oh, my God! You're so awesome!" Regan gushed.

I looked up to see Randy admiring an arrow on the target across the way that was just outside the bullseye and rewarding their team with nine points. The target was a white board with circular rings drawn on it with magic markers.

"I didn't know they had magic markers in medieval times," I said, gripping the bow.

"Yes, DaVinci invented them during the Renaissance period," the station supervisor said with a smirk.

"Making friends already, I see," Randy said.

I ignored him. As I grabbed an arrow and fumbled with it, trying to line the arrow up with the string on the nocking point, I heard Regan ask, "What's such a pretty girl like you doing with a nerd like him?"

I wasn't sure if she was trying to knock me off my game or was genuinely interested in one of life's great mysteries. I tried to block it out as I put all my focus on the arrow. I finally got it set up properly and pulled back the string, eyeing the target.

Sophie responded, "Well, after dating and dumping Randy, I realized that I was a proud member of Nerd Nation."

I unleashed my first arrow as Regan started yelling, "You didn't tell me you dated her!"

"We've been together for a week! What do you want, my whole life history?" Randy said, angrily.

Just Charles yelled, "Nerd Nation!"

I held up my bow and yelled, "Huzzah!" And then realized that my arrow had missed. I didn't even see it anywhere.

"Let's go while they're busy!" Sophie said. "We have nine more arrows."

I looked over to see Ben licking the tip of the suction-cupped arrow. I nearly threw up in my mouth. I lined up another arrow and let it fly, missing high. Like really high.

Like I think I may have shot a hawk out of the sky. At least I hit something.

"A little lower," Sophie said, unhelpfully.

"Trying," I said, a touch annoyed.

I lined up another shot and focused on the target. As I was about to unleash my third arrow, I felt something pelt me in the temple. I tried to hold onto the string, but couldn't as it slipped through my fingers, flubbing the shot. It arced briefly and then killed a worm about ten feet before the target.

"Hey, they're cheating!" I yelled, pointing at Randy and Regan.

"Just keep going. Two more and then we switch," Sophie said. "Knock it off, Randy. Can't you ever win in a fair fight?" Sophie yelled at him.

I reached for another arrow in the bucket and only felt two. I looked down to see a bunch of arrows missing.

"Hey!" I yelled. "We had ten. I only shot three, but we only have two left!"

Sir Thaddeus walked up, his brow furrowed.

I looked at him and said, "They stole our arrows!"

Randy responded quickly, "We did not. He shot a ton of them into the woods. He's terrible!" Randy barely looked at the target, let his arrow rip, and scored an eight.

Sir Thaddeus looked at Randy and said, "An un-noble knight is no knight at all."

"That's helpful. Thank you," Randy said, lining up another shot.

Sophie held out her hand and said calmly, but firmly, "Give it here."

I handed the bow to Sophie and backed away. She was going into the Sophie zone. I had seen it a few times before, most notably when Luke and a former band member of ours, Sly, said that girls couldn't rock out on the guitar. She made them look stupid.

Randy hit his final target. The station supervisor made a note on his clipboard and then reached into a black pouch, seemingly to pay out the four jewels.

"We only have two shots to get fifty points or we have to wait for them to gather the arrows in the next round. That's two bullseyes," I said to Sophie.

"Thank you for that information," Sophie said, almost robotic.

I took a deep breath. Randy and Regan took off, laughing. I tried to trip him, but missed. Ugh. He was going to be miles ahead of us. Sophie wasn't even paying attention to me. She was in the Sophie Zone. She unleashed an arrow with authority. It soared through the air, seemingly a bit high, but it hit its peak and began to fall. I held my breath as the arrow crushed the bullseye with a pop.

"Huzzah!" I yelled, and then handed Sophie another arrow.

Sophie grabbed the arrow without a word, lined it up, and let it rip. It soared through the air, almost a carbon copy of the first, and popped the bullseye right next to the first shot. My eyes popped out of my head.

15

B en, Ditzy Dayna, Sir Thaddeus, the station supervisor, and I all stood there in shock.

"Can we have our jewels?" Sophie asked the station supervisor.

"Umm, yes. Of course," he said, lifting his clipboard.

Sir Thaddeus looked at me and then Sophie, "Holy cannoli. Err, your performance was extraordinary, my lady."

Sophie was all business. She didn't even respond to him. She looked at me and said, "Let's go to the riddle station next. We can pick up some jewels without having to do anything physical."

"I feel like that's directed at me," I called out as Sophie started running.

She never answered. She read the map as she ran and I still had trouble keeping up with her. Ditzy Dayna was also ahead of Ben and me. It was the tights. I was sure of it.

As we approached the riddle station, there were a handful of kids there. All of them looked perplexed. So, it was basically like another day at Cherry Avenue Middle School.

The supervisor handed Sophie and me a rolled-up piece of paper, tied with a bow.

"Aww, how cute," she said, handing it to me.

I unrolled the parchment and read it out loud. "You are a trader of goods, stuck at an impasse. You stand on the edge of a river bank with a small raft, a sheep, a wolf, and a bushel of cabbage. You can only take one across the river with you at a time. Leaving the sheep with the wolf on either side will surely end in the sheep's demise. Leave the sheep with the cabbage and it will surely eat your prize, leaving you with no cabbage, but a stinky surprise. How can you get all three safely across? Receive two points for the correct answer." I looked at Sophie and said, "What do you think?"

"Well, we can't leave the sheep with the wolf or the cabbage, so why not bring the sheep across first?" Sophie said.

"Okay. It didn't say anything about leaving the wolf with the cabbage. Then we go back and take what? If we bring the wolf across and leave it with the sheep, it's mutton for lunch, and if we bring the cabbage, the sheep is gonna fart up a storm."

Sophie laughed and then furrowed her brow. "It's seemingly impossible. The sheep can never be left with either. And you can only take one across at a time."

"Hmm," I said. "You can only take one across at a time," I repeated, thinking. "It doesn't say which way."

"What do you mean?"

"Well, you can't leave the sheep with either of the others, so what if you kept it away from both?"

Sophie thought about it for a second. "How?"

"You drop off the sheep, leaving the wolf and the cabbage behind."

"Ok, good there."

"Then you go back for the wolf, bring it across. But instead of leaving the wolf and the sheep together, you take the sheep back with you, and then swap it with the cabbage?"

"That's it! Then you leave the wolf and cabbage together and go back for the sheep."

I finished the plan, "And then you'll have all three on the other side, never having left the sheep with either of the other two."

Sophie jumped and hugged me. "You're so smart!"

I didn't have time to get embarrassed. She grabbed me by the hand and pulled me to the station supervisor. We whispered our answer, got our two jewels, and then he handed us another piece of parchment.

He said, "Answer this and you get one more jewel."

I grabbed it and we found a quiet spot off to the side. I opened the parchment and read, "An old knight greeted a young squire as follows: 'May you live long – as long again as you have lived so far, and as long again as your age would be then, and then to three times that age and you will be ninety-nine years old.' How old was the squire at the time?"

"So, how do we do this?" She asked.

I looked at the riddle again. "Well, there are too many combinations if you start from how old he is at the beginning. We'd just be guessing."

"But we know how old he ends up, so we can work backwards, right?"

"Bingo," I said.

"I don't think they said 'bingo' in medieval times," Sophie said.

"I don't think they had suction cups for arrows, either. Now, if we work backwards, we've got ninety-nine and it said to multiply by three times. So, dividing that, we get thirty-three."

"And it was a double before that, right?" Sophie asked.

"Yep, so sixteen and a half. And another double before that."

"So, eight and a quarter."

"Which is eight and three months. Let's go!"

We rushed back to the station, told the supervisor our answer, and got another jewel. We had seven, which meant we only needed five more. We had to be at least tied with Randy, if not ahead.

As we ran, I looked over to see Ben pulling his hair out as Ditzy Dayna counted on her fingers. I wanted to yell, "Told ya so!" But didn't.

16

It was jousting time. I breathed a sigh of relief as we ran up to the station. I didn't have to ride a bike and there were no bodies of water anywhere to be found. There were two wooden beams opposite each other, running above our heads with rings hanging from little hooks. There were garbage pails (Were there plastic garbage pails during medieval times?) filled with jousting lances and another with plush stuffed animal horse head on a stick. All of the kids who were trying to snag the rings held the horse stick between their legs as they galloped along the path.

I've embarrassed myself worse than that in front of Sophie. Like almost daily. I grabbed a lance and a horse. It whinnied as I picked it up. It was going to be fun. Sophie was right behind me, lance and horse in hand. I was sure she didn't practice at all, but would be racking up rings left and right. And helping my nerdy butt to victory.

I waited my turn. There was a line of kids in front of me, waiting to go while others ran past on the other side.

Just Charles came through with a "Huzzah!" as he saw

me, but had no rings on his lance. "I stink!" he added with a smile.

Cheryl Van Snoogle-Something was right behind Just Charles, as I readied to go. She smiled as she passed, three rings on her lance.

The supervisor in front of me stepped out of my path and said way too enthusiastically, "Ride, Sir Knight! Ride!"

I wore my bag on my back, held my stick horse with my left hand and steadied my lance with my right, as I galloped like an idiot, heading toward the first ring. My eyes locked in on it. The tip of my lance bounced up and down as I trotted, but I kept it close to center. I slowed just a touch as I approached the first ring and split the middle of the hole! The ring clanked as my lance pulled it from the hook and continued on to the next one.

I lined the jousting lance up again and encircled another ring. And then another. I couldn't believe how well I was doing.

I yelled to Sophie, "This is so easy!" And then promptly missed the fourth ring.

I continued on, refocused on the final ring. I pretended it was a bubble hanging from the hook. With a thrust of my lance, I stabbed the center of the ring and continued riding my noble stick steed. The ring clanked onto the lance, landing on top of the other three. I thrust the lance into the air with a "Huzzah!"

I was ecstatic landing four out of the five rings. Based on the clanking going on behind me, Sophie was racking them up, too. Before I could even properly celebrate with Sophie, my feet stumbled over something. My body surged forward, off balance. I tried to stay on my feet, which just made my ultimate crash that much worse. I stumbled a few more feet and then smacked right into Amanda Gluskin's butt. I felt like a crash-test dummy driving into a wall. My face connected with her butt with a splat. I bounced back, stunned, and fell on my own butt.

I looked up to see Randy, Regan, Nick DeRozan, and others laughing. Blood surged to my face. I wasn't sure if it was because I was embarrassed or that's what happened when you head-butted (no pun intended) a brick wall. I sat there amid the laughter, catching my breath. I tossed the stupid stick horse to the side and dropped my lance.

Sophie came up from behind me and asked, "Are you okay?"

"Yeah," I said, rubbing my face. "I don't know what happened. I just tripped."

"Yeah, over Randy's lance. I saw him trip you with it," Sophie said, angrily.

I stood up fully and stormed at Randy. "Do you ever

know how to play fair? Cheater!" I bumped him with my chest. Not exactly the smartest of moves, even if it was only Randy there. But Nick DeRozan was there, too, and his breakfast steak was bigger than me. And I think he ate it raw.

Randy put his arm around me and patted me on the back. "Let me tell you something, Davenfart. The rules don't apply to me. I do what I want, when I want. The sooner you understand that, the better off you'll be." He pated me on the shoulder and then pushed me back with both hands. I stumbled a few feet, but was back in his face in no time.

One of the station supervisors rushed to us, yelling, "Hey, knock it off!" He separated us, holding us apart with his hands. "Time to move on. It's just a game."

Randy said, "I'm cool, man. No worries." And then he reached for his neck and then looked down on the ground, surprised. He said frantically, "Where are my jewels? My jewels are missing! Somebody stole my jewels!" Randy pointed to me. "It was him! Check him. He challenged me in this quest and now he's cheating because he can't win!"

The station supervisor remained calm. "Why don't we look around for a bit before we start accusing people of cheating?"

"Check him. I know it was him!"

"I saw him reach back behind his head. He probably put it in his bag," Regan added, unhelpfully.

Out of nowhere, Ben stepped in front of me. "He didn't steal anything. Randy's the cheater."

"Then you'll have no problem surrendering your bag?" Randy asked me.

"I don't care. I didn't touch your jewels," I said.

Sophie looked at me and mouthed, "We should run."

I looked at her confused as I handed the bag to the

supervisor. Did she cheat and take his jewels? She never would've done that. Or did Randy plant them on us? That was more like it, but before it all computed, the man had already dumped my bag, spilling an even smaller bag of jewels onto the ground.

"That's not mine," I said.

"Of course, they're not!" Randy yelled. "They're mine! You stole them! Arrest them!"

Sophie and Ben stepped in front of me. "This is ridiculous!" Sophie yelled. "He's acting!"

"You're all heading to the dungeon!" the station supervisor yelled.

17

I stared at the station supervisor and said, "Okay. If that's what you think is best." I leaned down and grabbed my stick horse. "It'll be a quicker ride on this."

"Okay," he said, like I was a weirdo or something.

Sophie and I looked at each other for a moment before we both screamed at each other, "Run!"

I threw my horse at Randy and the supervisor and took off behind Sophie. I looked back over my shoulder to see that Ben and Ditzy Dayna were on my heels, and the station supervisor was only a few steps behind them. We were nerds, so we were not likely going to outrun anyone our own age, but he was a big dude and probably only a few years younger than my parents. Ben and I had a shot at winning. We'd better, because otherwise we'd rot in the dungeon.

We ran through the crowds as quickly and quietly as we could. Sophie was a good ten feet ahead of me. I saw her cut around the dirty water cart and then disappear.

I called to Ben and Ditzy Dayna, "Follow her!"

We cut around the cart, ducking as we ran. I searched

frantically for Sophie and eventually saw her waving to me from underneath the tent flap at Lady Tabitha's Fortune Telling. I dove in as Sophie dropped the flap behind us. We rolled to a stop, Ben and Ditzy Dayna on top of me.

"I think we lost him," Sophie said.

"I think I lost my face and my spleen. Do people even have spleens?"

"I don't see your spleen anywhere and didn't see him as you were heading in," Sophie said.

"Hello, down there," a familiar female voice said. "I knew you would be back."

I wiped the sweat from my brow and looked up. Mr. Gifford, still in his full chainmail, and Lady Tabitha sat at the table across from each other.

Mr. Gifford looked at me and gave me a clanky thumbs up. "She says I'll find love again!"

Ben helped me up from the ground.

"Good news, sir," I said, not as excited as I normally would've been.

"Is everything okay?" he asked.

"Well," I said, looking at Lady Tabitha. "Let's just say no heroes have been born just yet, but revenge is on the way."

Mr. Gifford stood up. "That sounds lovely. I've gotta head back. There's a big Protectors meet and greet. Lady Dionisia the Deadly could be the one!"

"Good luck," I said with a thumbs up.

Sophie looked out from the tent and said, "It looks clear."

Mr. Gifford stepped out of the tent with us and immediately, I knew it was a mistake. Four armored guards jumped out from the side of the tent with swords at the ready.

One of them yelled, "Surrender or die!"

"Umm, yes. We'll surrender," I said, hoping that pee wouldn't start gushing from my tights.

"Oh, not you, kid. I was talking to Sir whatever his name is here."

"Me? What is going on? I'm a Protector!"

Two guards grabbed Mr. Gifford by each arm and pulled him away.

"Unhand me!" Mr. Gifford yelled, as the guards dragged him.

"What the heck just happened?" Sophie asked.

Ditzy Dayna shrugged and said, "Do we know him?"

Ben nearly fell over and then looked up at the sky. "Why?"

Before any of us could offer any ideas, Sammie burst from the crowd, tears streaming down her face.

"Sammie! Over here!" Sophie called.

"What's wrong?" I asked. "Where's Derek?"

"It's...Derek," she said through tears.

"What happened?" I asked, concerned.

"He turned...to the...dark side."

"What?" Sophie asked.

I grabbed Sammie's shoulders. "This isn't Star Wars. What are you talking about?" And I was already pretty sure he was already on the dark side.

"He joined...with Butt Hair...and overthrew...the Protectors!"

"What?" Sophie asked. She was asking really good questions.

"I thought...he liked me."

"He does," I said, not knowing if it was actually the case. "Take a deep breath. Tell us what happened."

Sammie wiped her eyes while Sophie pulled her hair

back. Sammie took a deep breath and exhaled. "Principal Butt Hair brought his own army."

"What?" we all asked.

"Those guys that got Mr. Gifford must have taken all of the Protectors!" Ben said.

"Where did you see Derek last?" I asked.

"I left him in the great hall after they took over. They're taking the prisoners to the center of town. Principal Butt Hair is going to give a speech or something."

"What are we going to do?" Sophie asked.

"I was thinking of getting a turkey leg," Ditzy Dayna said.

"Maybe later," Ben said, rolling his eyes.

"We're going to lose the quest," I said, looking at Sophie.

"We need to stop them," Sophie said.

"We shall defeat them!" I said, raising my fist in the air. "Huzzah!"

WE HID in the shadows of the town, staring out toward the stockades on the platform in the town center. There were four guards surrounding the platform. People were scattering about, not sure of what was going on.

"Make way for the prisoners!" Derek yelled from afar, in his deepest voice possible.

I craned my neck to see Derek leading a group of four prisoners and five guards up onto the platform. My stomach churned when I saw that the prisoners were Mr. Gifford, Sir Thaddeus and Lord Dinkledorf, and Zorch.

Derek nodded to the guards already on the platform and said, "Lock 'em up."

The guards grunted and opened the stockades. The

second group of guards lined the prisoners up in front of the open stockades and then forced them forward. All of the prisoners' heads and arms were locked in the wooden stockade. Lord Dinkledorf looked out into the crowd, anger on his face.

And then trumpets blared. The crowd moved back, away from the platform. All of the guards except for Derek hopped off, making way for a new group of people. The two trumpeters and the official-looking announcer dude from the great hall stepped up on the platform.

The announcer, looking less than enthused, stood in front of the crowd, straightened his clothes, and cleared his throat. He revealed a rolled-up piece of parchment. He opened it and shook his head.

In a monotone voice, he read, "For the greater good of The Realm, these traitorous Protectors have been arrested. The remaining Protectors unanimously voted Sir Simon the Serious as Emperor of the Realm."

Chatter grew amongst the crowd. Worry spread across the onlookers. Old ladies and babies cried.

"Why?"

"Traitors? Never!"

"Emperor?"

The announcer continued, "All hail the Emperor."

Principal Buthaire stepped onto the stage, his shoulders thrust back and his nose in the air. The crowd was stunned to silence.

Principal Buthaire nodded to Derek and said, "He needs a little more enthusiasm."

Derek drew his sword and held it under the chin of the announcer. "Pretend like you mean it."

The announcer gulped and then cleared his throat again. "I said, 'All hail the emperor!'"

Derek pointed his sword at a few people in the front of the crowd, who repeated, "All hail the emperor!" and bowed.

Principal Buthaire looked at the announcer and said, "Thank you, my loyal servant. Such a fine speech. I'm not surprised. It was I who wrote it." He looked at the crowd. "Welcome, my loyal subjects. How exciting this must be for you to meet your Emperor. I envy you. Well, you're peasants and I'm the Emperor, so that 'tis but a lie to make you feel good about your lowly selves."

As the Emperor continued his humble speech, Just Charles ran up to us, huffing and puffing. Cheryl Van

Snoogle-Something was right beside him. We all waited for him to say something, but it was taking so long for him to catch his breath that he pointed to Cheryl.

Cheryl shook her head and said, "He wanted you to know that Randy has ten jewels already. He only needs two more to complete the crown."

"We have bigger problems that that," I said, pointing to Emperor Buthaire.

"What the-" Just Charles said, finally catching his breath and looking over at the prisoners and the new Emperor.

"We need to talk to the prisoners," I said.

"How the heck are we gonna do that?" Sophie asked. "The guards are going to snatch us up in two seconds."

Ben added, "How long do you think it'll take before Buthaire puts out a warrant for your arrest?"

"He's the Sheriff now, too?" I asked. But he made a good point. If Principal Buthaire was the Emperor of the Realm. I was enemy of the Realm number one.

And within seconds, Sophie and Ben were proven right. Derek stepped forward to the edge of the platform.

He used his deep voice again and yelled, "By the Emperor's orders, I hereby declare that a warrant for arrest has been issued for the following traitors: Sir Austin Davenport, Lady Sophie Rodriguez, Sir Benjamin Gordon, Lady Ditzy Dayna, Sir Charles Blank, Lady Cheryl Van Snoogle-Something, Sir Luke Hill, and Lady Kami Rahm."

We all looked at each other, fear seeping from our pores.

Ditzy Dayna looked at us and said, "This is exciting!"

18

The crowd around the prisoners was still pretty thick and none of them knew us, so we decided we were safer in the crowd than not. Derek paced around the outer edge of the platform, supervising the guards who watched the locked-up prisoners. It was all riveting stuff.

Derek called out, "No one may approach the prisoners unless they choose to humiliate them. Those are the Emperor's orders!"

"We need to take Derek out of the equation," I said.

"We can distract him, but we also need a disguise," Sophie said.

"What about those wizard hats with the attached beards?" Ben asked. "They sold them at one of the shops."

"Good idea," I said.

"I'll get the wizard hat," Just Charles said and took off with Cheryl Van Snoogle-Something.

"Who's going up to talk to the prisoners?" I asked.

Ben said, "I'm not doing it. Just Charles probably won't, either."

"I'll do it," Sophie said.

"No, I will." I looked at Sophie and said, "You probably would look better in the beard than me, but I got us into this mess. I should go."

"It's riskier with Derek up there," Ben said.

"Not with the proper diversion," I said, looking at Sammie.

Just Charles and Cheryl returned with a wizard hat and attached white beard. He handed it to me and said, "You owe me twelve bucks."

"I'll pay you back." I slipped on the wizard hat.

Sophie stood in front of me and adjusted my beard.

"How do I look?" I asked

"You look so old," Sophie said, laughing.

I puckered up my lips. "Give your old Grandpa a big kiss," I said in my best Grandpa voice.

"Over my dead body, Grandpa," Sophie said, pushing me away playfully.

"Okay, we need to move," Ben said.

I looked at Sammie and said, "Sammie, maybe you should talk to Derek and see what's going on? I'm sure there's a reasonable explanation for all of this." I was pretty sure there wasn't, but she would be a good distraction.

Sammie nodded and said, "You think so?" She had hope in her eyes. I immediately felt bad.

"It's worth a try," I said, with a shrug. He's not always a horrible human being. Just most of the time.

Sammie walked toward Derek. I branched off from her and cut through the crowd.

I stopped at the edge of the crowd and surveyed the situation. Most of the guards were staring out into space, not paying any attention to what was going on and Sammie was absorbing all of Derek's attention.

A little girl stood in front of the prisoners, putting lipstick on them.

I stepped up onto the stage and walked toward Lord Dinkledorf.

A voice behind me asked, "What are you doing?"

I didn't turn around. I just pointed at the little girl who was prettying up Zorch's face.

"I'm with her."

"Oh, okay."

I walked over to Lord Dinkledorf and bent down in front of him. He looked at me quizzically through glazed-over eyes. His lips sparkled with pink-glittered lipstick. I pulled down my beard for a quick second, revealing my face.

Lord Dinkedorf's eyes lit up. "You're in grave danger, Sir Austin. But more important, how do I look in this lipstick?"

I chuckled and then asked, "Are you okay, sir?"

I glanced over to see the guard eyeing me suspiciously.

I looked at Lord Dinkledorf. "I'm gonna have to smack you now." I slapped him across the face and then gave the guard a thumbs up. He smiled.

I looked back at Lord Dinkledorf and whispered, "Sorry, sir."

"No, totally fine."

"We have to get you out of here, but how?"

"We have to defeat Butt Hair's army," Lord Dinkledorf said with disgust.

"Do you call him that?"

"Today, I do. He brought his own army and overthrew the Protectors!"

I felt the platform shake. A guard was walking toward us. I whispered, "Sorry, sir," and smacked Lord Dinkledorf again across the face. "Traitor!" I yelled.

"Nice one, old man," the guard said, walking by me.

I whispered to Lord Dinkledorf, "How can we free you and take them out?"

"Don't. Get the dragon's egg and win," he said.

"But how?" I asked.

I heard Sophie's voice from behind me say, "Run!"

I looked around and saw the jousting station supervisor heading my way with Randy and Regan right behind him.

"There he is!" Randy yelled. "The cheater! Seize him!"

"Hey, that's my job!" Derek yelled and then, "Seize him!" Derek looked around. "Why are we seizing that old guy?"

Randy hopped up onto the platform. I stood up and backed away.

"Back off, Warblemacher or you just might find yourself in the dungeon!" Derek yelled. "I'm the Sheriff of these here parts." I think he got medieval times and the Wild West mixed up for a minute there.

A guard stepped toward Randy. "Stand down, boy."

Randy did the opposite of Derek and took the medieval thing a little too far. "You would be wise to hold your tongue, guard, forthe heretofore stands beforeth you the future prince of The Realm!"

The guard didn't appear to know what to do. I remembered the wise words of my girlfriend, who told me to run. So, I did. Right into a giant guard who engulfed me in his hulking arms. He did smile, though.

"Cheaters!" Randy yelled again.

I struggled to get loose, but it was no use. He was too big and I was too much of a nerd. And then my breath seemed to be sucked from my lungs. I wasn't sure if it was because the guard was trying to pop my ribs like bubble wrap or because all of my friends had been captured, too.

The jousting station supervisor yelled, "Cheaters rot in the dungeon!"

Derek whined, "Man, that's my job," and then yelled in his deep voice, "To the dungeon!"

Randy smiled like an idiot and then ran off, Regan on his heels.

The guards dragged us through the crowds. People stopped and watched. Some waved. It was nice. We really got to meet a lot of new people. We'd never see them again because we were going to rot in the dungeon, but still.

"Where are you taking us?" Ditzy Dayna asked.

The guard answered, "It's the dungeon for you, peasants!"

"That's hurtful," I said.

"Let us go!" Sophie yelled.

The guard pushed Sophie from behind. She stumbled forward, but stayed on her feet.

"Hey! That's my girlfriend!" I yelled, as I thrust my elbow into the gut of the guard behind me.

"Oww!" we both yelled.

The guard grabbed me and laughed, "It's the chains for you, peasant."

"Huh? What chains?"

The guards led us into a small, wooden building and through a dark, narrow hallway. A door creaked open. One by one, they pushed us into the dimly-lit room. I was last. My guard followed me in. I tripped over something and found myself on the floor next to the rest of the crew.

The guard said, "This is gonna be easier than I thought. Chain yourself up." He nodded to me.

"Or what?" I asked.

"Or I do it myself, but your arms won't be attached to the rest of your body, peasant boy."

I grabbed the chains. "This way is good." I slapped them onto my wrists and held them up for the guard to lock them.

The guard held out a key and locked the chains around my wrists. He turned and started to leave.

Ditzy Dayna asked, "Can you order us some turkey leg takeout?"

"Yeah," the guard nodded with a smirk. "It'll be here in thirty minutes."

"Sweet! Thanks."

"Oh, you should know," the guard said, "there are clues that can help you escape. Otherwise, you get out in an hour."

"An hour!" I yelled.

The guard closed the doors. The lock turned with a clank. I looked at our crew. It was Sophie, Ben, Ditzy Dayna, Sammie, and me.

Sophie said, "Randy will have won by then."

Ben said, "Worse than that, Butt Hair and Derek will have taken over the universe by then!"

"Just Charles and Cheryl Van Snoogle-Something evaded capture! Perhaps they will come to our rescue," I said, hopefully.

And then I looked down at the chains on my wrists and felt less hopeful. I followed the chains to where they connected to the wall. There was a wooden panel with giant eye hooks holding the chains. I pulled on the chains as hard as I could. They didn't budge.

"Okay," I said, "We're in a bit of trouble here. Any ideas?"

"I'm fresh out," Ben said.

"There's a loose brick over here," Sophie said, squatting down in the corner of the room. "It's just kinda hanging out of the wall."

Sammie sat in the opposite corner, whispering to herself, "My prince, my sweet prince."

"Umm, Sammie? When was he ever sweet?" Sophie asked. She was the best.

"Remember when he almost knocked me out with the football?" Sammie asked, as if remembering the best moment of her life.

"Yeah, he's a real knight in shining armor," Ben said.

"So, we have a brick," I said, trying to get the conversation back on our escape. "What else? A key? A clue of any type?"

"Nope," Ben said.

"Nada," Sophie added.

'In half an hour, we're gonna have turkey legs," Ditzy Dayna said.

I exhaled slowly. "That's it. We lost," I said, frustrated. "I lost again to Randy. Do you think we could get all of our families to move to Bear Creek?"

"They don't even have a Starbucks," Sammie whimpered.

20

We were doomed, well, at least for another fifty-eight minutes or so until they let us out. And then we were going to lose to Randy, Derek, and Emperor Butt Hair. I laid my head down on the floor and looked up at the ceiling. My eyes bulged wide open.

"Guys, er, lords and ladies. We have a window," I said.

The crew looked up above us and let out a collective, "Huzzah!"

"Let's build a human ladder!" Ditzy Dayna said.

"That's actually a decent idea," Ben said.

"I'll guide you. I can't do anything with these chains."

"Even if we escape, Austin's still going to be stuck," Sophie said.

"We can break out from the window and then steal the keys from the guard and then get you out," Ben said.

"I don't see how that's going to work, but at least you guys will escape," I said. "Ben, you're the base. Dayna will climb up next and then Sophie."

"Okay," Ben said, softly.

Ben leaned up against the wall underneath the window.

"Squat down. Get some bend in your legs, so they can use that to step on and climb up," I said.

"Good idea," Ben said. He followed my advice.

Dayna stood behind him, her hands on his shoulders while she looked up at the window.

Ben gritted his teeth. "I don't...know how...much longer...I can hold this!"

"Dayna hasn't even started climbing yet!" Sophie said.

"This is exhausting," Ben whispered as he crumpled to the ground.

"We're never getting out of here," I said.

"Guys, I've got it," Dayna said, excited. "All we need is an axe to hack down that door."

"Yeah, we have no axe," I said, wanting to knock myself out with the chains.

"That's okay. Let's just hook up some horses or, even better, some oxen to pull the bars off the window!" Dayna yelled.

"That's awesome," I said. "Great idea, but one problem. We're in here. And we have no oxen."

"Can we get out there and then find some oxen to hook up to the window?"

"How are we going to get out to get the oxen?" I asked.

"Why are you even bothering?" Sophie asked.

Ditzy Dayna said, "Let's tunnel out of here. Does anybody have a rock hammer or a shovel?"

"Does it look like it? Oh, my goodness," Sophie said.

"See? It's hard to keep quiet, right?" I asked Sophie.

She nodded, her face somber.

"What's that over there?" I asked, pointing. There were letters written with chalk or stone randomly across the stone wall.

Ben awoke from his coma, took a close look, and said,

"Just letters. There are too many of them. It makes no sense."

"Where did the brick come from?" I asked.

Sophie and Ben inspected the walls for a minute.

"Here," Sophie said. She kneeled down and peeked into the hole left by the missing brick. "I think there's something buried back there." Sophie reached in. "Yep." She shoveled out dirt with her hand before pulling out a wooden cylinder.

Sophie walked over to me, inspecting the cylinder. "What is this thing? It looks like a combination lock, only there are pictures on them." Sophie handed it to me.

I grabbed it and twisted it. "It's a cryptex like DaVinci talked about!"

"Too much nerd, dude. Even for me," Ben said. "What the heck is it? In regular people talk."

"Yeah, that would be helpful," Ditzy Dayna said.

I bit my tongue. "Well, it's exactly like Sophie said. It's a combination lock with pictures. DaVinci created it and called it a cryptex. It sounds a lot cooler than a combination lock with pictures."

"Yeah, it totally does," Ben said.

I studied the cryptex from every angle. "There are six symbols on it." I did some math in my head. "That's like thirteen hundred different combos. Even if we assumed you only use each symbol once, it's still...three hundred and sixty."

"How the heck do you do that?" Sophie asked.

"What?" I asked, blushing.

"You're like a calculator."

Ditzy Dayna grabbed her stomach and said, "I think I have to go to the bathroom."

Ben pounded on the door for a minute, but nobody came.

"It's okay," Dayna said. "It was just a fart."

"Great call, Ben," I said.

"I have to go again," Ditzy Dayna said. "Wait, nope I'm good."

"Did you fart again?"

"Yeah, I think I ate something funky."

"Oh, God! You're standing right in front of my face!" I yelled. I started to gag.

"It was the dirty water!" Ben said.

"Let's just open that window up there," Ditzy Dayna said.

"Need...air...life force...draining," I said, slumping over on my side. I felt my connection to the physical world slipping away. "Medieval farts are so much worse than modern farts."

"Knock it off, Austin," Sophie said, annoyed. "We have to figure a way out of here."

"Well, a way better than death by dirty water fart," I said.

"Seriously," Sophie said, shaking her head.

Perhaps I was exaggerating a smidge. "Sorry," I said, ashamed. I sat up and focused on the cryptex. "So, there's a shield, a heart, a scale weighing something, a horse, a person handing something to someone, and a castle." I held it up for Ben to look at. "I've got nothing. It can be any combo."

Ben grabbed it and spun some of the symbols around. "There's no way this is going to work. We need more clues."

"So, we have this brick," Sophie said, holding it up, "the cryptex, and some writing on the wall."

"Smash the crypex with the brick," Ditzy Dayna said.

"No way," I said. "Fart on it. The cryptex might surrender."

"Farting is natural," Ditzy Dayna said. "It's just air."

"Foul air," Ben whispered to me.

"The brick probably doesn't have anything to do with the puzzle. It was just hiding the cryptex," Sophie said, tossing it onto the floor.

The brick landed with a thud and a rattle.

Ben looked at me and asked, "Did you jiggle your chain?"

"No, I didn't move."

"I heard something," Ben said.

"Me, too," Sophie said, picking the brick back up and shaking it. There was a tiny clanking, like there was plastic or metal inside. She studied it side by side. She stopped and held it up to the light. "I think there's something in this crack." Sophie took the brick over to the wall. She smacked it against the wall at an angle. She looked at the brick again and smiled. "Surprise," she said as she pulled a small, metal key out of the brick.

"Uncuff me!" I said, enthusiastically.

Sophie rushed over to me and pushed the key into the lock. She frowned as she tried to turn it. The key wouldn't budge. "This isn't the right key."

I exhaled, frustrated. Maybe Dayna should fart on the chains. I wondered if the chains would vaporize into thin air.

"Try the door," Ben said.

Sophie stood up and said, "Good idea," as she walked over to the door. She tried to push the key in, but it wouldn't even fit, let alone turn. "That didn't work, either."

"What the heck does it work on?" I asked.

Nobody answered. We were all stumped.

Sophie paced around on the dirt floor. She stopped abruptly and looked down at the ground, her brow furrowed. She pressed on the ground with her foot, intrigued by what was beneath it.

"What is it?" I asked.

"This isn't dirt. It has some give to it. I think it's wood. It's kind of bending under my weight."

Ben rushed over to help Sophie dig. I was also able to help pull away some of the dirt with my hands and chains. Sammie didn't budge from the corner. I knew she'd eventually be okay, but I felt bad that my brother was such an idiot. Nobody understood how much of an idiot he was more than I did.

After a few minutes of digging and removing dirt from above the soft spot, Sophie dug her fingers into the hole. She lifted up a wooden rectangle board about an inch thick, a foot long and two feet wide. Sophie tossed it aside as she and Ben both peered down into the hole.

"What is it?" I asked, eagerly.

"It's a box," Ben said.

"Maybe the key will work on this," Sophie said, pulling the box out of the ground and placing it at my feet.

Sophie plugged the key into the box. It slid in quickly. She turned it and the latch popped open.

"Huzzah!" I yelled.

Sophie opened the box, removed a ratty towel and tossed it to Ben, and then lifted a small wooden puzzle out of it.

"What the heck?" Sophie said.

Ben spread the towel out with both hands. It was littered with holes. "This looks like it must actually be from the medieval ages," Ben said, tossing it aside.

"What do you have, Soph?" I asked.

"It's a puzzle, some sort of maze."

She moved it next to me so that the three of us could all

examine it. There was a piece of metal stuck in a grooved track that appeared to be a maze. If we could get the metal through the maze, it seemed like we could get it out through an opening in the corner of the box.

I grabbed the metal and worked back from the exit in my mind. I found the right track and zig-zagged the metal through the maze until the piece popped out of the puzzle. I held it in my hand, not sure what it was.

"What is it?" Sophie asked.

"I don't know, besides metal. Let me take a closer look." I moved the metal closer to my eyes to get a better look. As I held it closer, the metal levitated from my hand and thrust toward my mouth. It connected with my teeth and braces with a smack.

"Oww!" I yelled, holding my mouth.

"What is it?" Ben asked.

I let out a muffled, "It's a magnet," from underneath my hands. I tossed it to him. "Keep that thing away from me," I said, rubbing my tooth. "It nearly broke my face!"

"Don't get so dramatic," Sophie said, laughing. "Are you okay?"

"Yes," I said, but then I had an idea. "Maybe they'll let us out of here with a medical emergency," I whispered.

"Yes!" Sophie said.

"Ham it up real good," Ben said.

"I was a lead in the hit musical, Santukkah! Just in case you don't remember."

"I remember you mooning the crowd, if you call that the lead," Ben said, chuckling. "More like the rear."

"That is a gross exaggeration. There was no mooning."

"It was definitely gross," Ben said.

I looked at Sophie. "A little help from my girlfriend, perhaps?"

"We weren't together at the time, so I'm staying out of it," she said, laughing.

"I'll try to get them to let us out and then we'll run," I said.

"Let's do this," Ben said, pounding his fist into his palm. It was a bit of an overreaction, but we needed some enthusiasm, so I didn't say anything.

I nodded at Sophie and said, "Ahh, my face, my face!"

"Guards! We need some help in here!" Sophie yelled, while pounding on the door.

That time, they heard us. Heavy footsteps pounded down the hall. Keys jiggled on the other side of the door. Sophie backed away as the door opened. I reached out and pulled the brick closer to me. I held my face and groaned.

The guard entered and looked around. He rushed to my side. "What's the matter?"

I didn't answer. I continued to groan.

"His face. It's horrible. The brick," Ben said.

"Let me see," the guard said, while trying to pull my hands away. I resisted.

"Unlock the chains and it won't be so cluttered," Sophie said.

The guard looked at Sophie. "Nice try," and then to me, "Lower your hands and let me see."

I squeezed my face, hoping to add some good redness to it before removing my hands.

The guard inspected my face. "Looks good," he said. "You still have about forty minutes ,unless you can escape before then." The guard stood up and headed for the door.

I looked at Sophie and Ben and yelled, "Run! Save yourselves!"

Ben took off like a bullet, well, as far as nerds are concerned, and ran straight for the door. The guard took one step to his left, completely blocking the door. Ben jumped into the air, leading with his shoulder. He connected with a thud and bounced off the guard's big belly. Ben fell to the ground, the guard barely interested.

"Nice try," the guard said, laughing. He closed the door and was gone.

21

I lay back with my head against the wooden beam. It was really comfy. Sophie slumped down onto the ground next to Sammie, who was still in the corner. Ben paced around, his chin in his hand.

Sophie patted Sammie's knee and whispered, "Are you doing okay?"

Sammie lifted her head and said, "I don't know. I'm a little cold. It's a little drafty in here."

Sophie furrowed her brow and asked, "Drafty how?" She put her hands up against the stone wall.

Sammie scooted out of the way and pointed to one of the stones. "It feels like there's some air coming out of there."

Sophie clawed at the stone, but didn't seem to move it at all. She traced her finger along the edge of the mortar. "There is definitely something behind this. It's not really concrete or whatever. This is a fake lining, but I can't get it out with my fingers."

"Great. Stuck again," Ben said, kicking the bunched-up

towel on the ground. The towel smacked the stone above my head and then fell on top of me.

"Hey!" I yelled, staring at Ben through one of the holes. Behind him, I saw the letters written on the wall. "Wait a minute." I pulled the towel off of my face and threw it at Ben as hard as I could as payback. Of course, I missed. I said, "Hold this up to the letters."

"What do you mean?" Ben asked.

Sophie hopped up, interested. Even Sammie was watching.

"I'm thinking the holes will narrow down the letters for a real clue."

"Ooh, I like it," Ben said, rushing to the letters. He held up the towel over the letters. He nodded at Sophie and said, "Here, take the other side."

Ben and Sophie held the towel over the letters while I read, "It spells, F-A-R-T."

"I already did and nothing happened!" Ditzy Dayna said. "Do you want me to do it again?"

"No!" we all yelled. Even Sammie joined in.

"Should somebody else fart then?" Ditzy Dayna asked. "Austin, Ben says you're pretty good at it."

I looked at Sophie and said, "I don't know what she's talking about," and then to the rest of the group, "That's a stinky clue. It doesn't make sense. Flip it over."

Ben and Sophie flipped the towel upside down, the holes in different places, revealing different letters. Both Ben and Sophie blocked me from seeing, as they leaned over in front of me, trying to read the letters.

"It spells B-A-R-D." Ben said. "What does the bard have to do with this?"

"What clue could the bard give us?" Sophie asked.

"What about his songs? Could there be clues in them?" I

asked. "Do you remember the songs?" I looked at Ben and started singing. "One need not be noble at birth. And then something about a castle, right?" I looked at the cryptex and moved the first combo piece to the castle. "What came next?"

Ben sang, "To take the castle and crown..."

Sophie said, "Try the crown. That's on the cryptex, right?"

"Yep," I said. "All I remember is the part about peeing. If we remember nothing else, that part was worth it. My bladder would be bursting right now."

"You must be noble in heart and show your worth!" Sophie said.

Ben paced around the prison cell, looking up at the ceiling. "It was noble in heart to show your worth. Hop on top of your noble steed and make sure that you've peed..."

"A steed is a horse!" Sophie said.

I clicked the next two pieces to the heart and the horse.

"Is there like a urinal on the cryptex or a toilet?" Ditzy Dayna asked.

"I don't think that's part of the clue," I said. I looked at the cryptex. "There's the person giving something to someone else and the scale. One side of the scale has something on it and is lower than the other."

"There's the journey to royalty. Those two don't seem to make sense," Ben said. "But..." Ben's eyes lit up. "But should you stray from chivalraaaaaay," he sang it like the bard, but with his voice cracking, "you'll be reduced to an average Joe and to the dungeon you will go!"

"Maybe the chivalry is the person giving something to the other?" I asked. "And the scale means being reduced in stature if you cheat?"

"Huzzah!" Sophie yelled.

I twisted the cryptex, lining up the chivalry picture and finally the scale. I took a deep breath and twisted the top. It popped open with a click. "Huzzah!"

"What's in it?" Ben asked, eagerly.

I took off the top of the cryptex and looked inside. It was dark in the room, but it looked like something long and thin. I turned the cryptex over. A thin bone slid out and poked the palm of my hand.

"It's sharp," I said, handing it to Sophie. "It looks like some sort of sharpened bone."

"Maybe we could use that to get at the fake mortar." Sophie said.

Sophie rushed over to Sammie and knelt down, inspecting the stones again. She took the bone and thrust it between two pieces of the stone. She used it as a lever and popped a piece of whatever it was out.

Ben grabbed it. "It's window caulk or something." He pulled it as Sophie continued to dig it out from between the stones.

When they were done, a three foot by three-foot square of stone had been disconnected from the rest of the wall.

"I think it's fake," Sophie said. She used the bone again as a lever and forced the piece from the rest of the wall. She dropped the bone and used her fingers to pull the stones away from the wall.

"Be careful, there might be dwarves back there," Ditzy Dayna said.

"I'll take my chances," Sophie said.

Ben joined Sophie and pulled the fake section away from the wall, revealing a dimly-lit tunnel.

"We're free!" Ben yelled.

"Huzzah!" I said.

Sophie looked at Sammie and said, "Come on, let's get you out of here."

Ben was first through the hole, then Dayna. Sophie helped Sammie up and then into the tunnel and followed her.

"Umm, guys?" I yelled. "I'm still locked in medieval chains here. Kind of a problem. They'll come back," I said to myself. I waited for a moment and then jiggled the chains. "Guys?"

Eventually, Ben and Sophie returned to the prison cell, one after the other. Ben shrugged, with a sheepish grin on his face.

"Oops," Sophie said, flashing her cutest smile.

"Oops? You left me to rot in prison with these chains!"

"It was like two minutes," Ben said.

"Sorry," Sophie said.

"Don't worry about it," I muttered, focused on my chains. The light from the tunnel illuminated the side of the wood panel that held the chains in place. It had a piece of glass imbedded in it. Behind it was something dark. And there was an opening above the glass.

"What is it?" Sophie asked.

"I don't know," I said, trying to get my fingers into the hole to grab whatever it was behind the glass. I couldn't fit my fingers in. "The magnet!"

Ben tossed it to me. Of course, I missed it, but I was glad that it connected with my chains and not my braces. I plucked it off the chain and held it up to the glass. The magnet sucked the concealed piece to it with a clink. I slid the magnet up to the top of the glass. The metal on the other side of the glass dangled from the magnet, as I slowly finagled it through the opening in the glass.

"Hang on, little buddy," I said.

I pulled the magnet out away from the glass. The concealed piece of metal teetered on top of the glass and then fully clinked against the magnet. I held both up in the air.

We all yelled, "Huzzah!"

I then realized I had no idea what it actually was that I pulled out of there. I looked at it and excitement surged through my veins.

"It's a key!"

22

I held the key in one of my shackled hands and took a deep breath. I didn't want to think about what would happen if it didn't work. I slid the key into the lock. It slipped in quickly. I closed my eyes and then turned the key. The shackle popped open with a click!

"I'm free!"

"We did it!" Sophie yelled.

I popped open the other lock and hopped up off the ground.

"Oh, God," I said.

"What?" Sophie asked, concerned.

"I think my butt fell asleep."

Ben stepped forward and slapped my butt. "That oughta wake it," he said, laughing.

"Oww! I got pins and needles in my tush!"

"Let's go!" Sophie said, diving into the tunnel.

Ben followed Sophie. I was right behind him.

"You didn't drink any of that dirty water, did you?" I asked.

Sophie and Ben laughed as we continued through the tunnel. I rammed Ben's butt as we came to a stop.

"Oww!"

"That was for the butt smack. It still hurts."

I leaned around Ben to see what Sophie was doing. She pushed on the wall in front of her. The wood creaked open like a door. Light burst into the tunnel. I blocked my eyes from the blinding sun, free at last. I followed Ben and Sophie out to find Ditzy Dayna and Sammie beside the exit.

Sammie hugged me, as I struggled to adjust to the light.

"We have to go," Sophie said.

"There's a path up ahead," Ben said.

I looked down the path. It appeared to lead back to the town center. I wondered what we would find when we got there, what evils the emperor and my brother had done since my incarceration. And if Randy had already been crowned the Prince of The Realm.

"But what do we do when we get there?" Sophie asked.

"We should save the Protectors," I said. "There's no way we can beat Randy at this point."

"There's one way," Sophie said. "We have to get the dragon's egg. That way we can win. I want you to win."

"They said it's never been done," I said.

"We'll be the first," Sophie said. "Do it for me. I know we can do this together."

I took a deep breath. "Okay," I said as confidently as I could. "To the Dragon's Keep!"

"Huzzah!"

"Oh, God. What is that smell?' Ben asked.

"Sorry. I farted during the huzzah," Ditzy Dayna said.

I stepped in front of Ben. "If Sophie and I go to the Dragon's Keep, you can free the Protectors."

"But how?" Ben asked.

"I don't know, but you've got to try. You're their only hope."

"You just Princess Leia-ed me."

"I did. You can't say no to a plea from Princess Leia."

Ben nodded. "Okay, Godspeed, Sir Austin." He looked at Sammie and Ditzy Dayna. "Follow me! And Dayna, stay in the back!"

They took off running, leaving Sophie and me alone with not much else but a map and a whole lot of fear and regret. I immediately wanted no part of the Dragon's Keep.

Sophie studied the map and ran her finger down a winding path. "It's deep into the forest. It's not too far from those stables there. We've got to hurry."

SOPHIE and I stood outside the Dragon's Keep, which, from the outside, only consisted of two wooden bilco doors that I guessed opened to stairs leading underground. It was quiet, which made sense because nobody in their right mind would even think about going in there. Sir Thaddeus had said that no one had ever made it out of there with the egg.

"Are you ready?" Sophie asked.

"I think so," I said and exhaled. "You?"

"Same. Let's do this," she said, enthusiastically.

"Huzzah!" I yelled.

Just as we were ready to go in, there was a boom followed by a crash. The wooden doors of the Dragon's Keep burst open. Nick DeRozan and Amanda Bradley surged from the Keep like the whole place was on fire. The doors slammed shut behind them. I wasn't sure which of them had the higher-pitched scream as they ran toward us.

My heart pounded as they ran past us, not even aware that we were there. They ran off into the woods, never to be seen again. Just kidding. They both lived happily ever after in the Cherry Avenue Home for Disturbed Children until their twenty-first birthdays.

Anyway, Sophie and I looked at each other, fear seeping from our pores.

"So, wanna go get a turkey leg and some dirty water to wash it down?" The dirty water and stomach bug that was likely to follow was a serious upgrade from our current plan. I looked at Sophie. Uh, oh. I had seen that look on her face before. And it wasn't her hungry face.

"No. A boy becomes a hero. A girl becomes a legend. We can still beat Randy and Regan! To the Dragon's Keep!" Sophie yelled, as she ran toward the Keep, leaving me in a cloud of dust, fear, and confusion.

I was super nervous, but I wasn't about let her go down there by herself. If she wanted to be a princess, I was going to do my best to be a prince. Or at least not her jester, which was pretty much every other day of my life.

Sophie stood outside the Keep, staring at me. "Are you coming?"

I nodded reluctantly and then jogged over to her. I reached down and grabbed the handle of the door and pulled. I almost broke my back. I don't think that was supposed to be part of the challenge.

I almost said, "Ladies first," but it wasn't a time for chivalry.

It was dark, but the sunlight showed us a stone stairwell that led down into the Keep, which must've been an old wine cellar or some sort of underground storage area back in the day. It was dark and smelled pretty gross.

I walked slowly down the stairs. Halfway down, I stopped and turned back. "If we don't make it out of here alive, being your boyfriend has been my life's greatest pleasure."

Sophie smiled and said, "I feel the same way...about turkey legs."

"Hey!"

She laughed, as she grabbed my hand and followed me down into the darkness of the Dragon's Keep. Never to return. Okay, I may be exaggerating. Or not.

23

The stairway led into a seemingly quiet room. We waded knee deep into loose straw, which appeared to cover the entire length of the floor. It seemed like a fire hazard to have all that straw in the Dragon's Keep, but whatever. We held hands as we walked slowly. There was scorched armor laying to our left and a skeleton beneath it. There were random bones sticking up from the straw throughout the room.

The hair stood up on the back of my neck. My knees were knocking. I squeezed Sophie's hand a little tighter. I squinted my eyes in the darkness and saw the outline of a doorway.

I whispered, "I think we need to go through there."

Sophie nodded. I could feel her hand shaking.

"Are you okay?" I asked.

"It's a lot easier to be confident when you're outside the Dragon's Keep," she whispered.

Without warning, something clamped onto my ankle and squeezed.

Sophie screamed and grabbed my arm. "Austin! Help!"

"Ahhh!" I yelled. Some might say it was similar to a baby's shriek after his candy was taken away. Times one thousand. "Something's got me!" I instinctively kicked, trying to shake loose and then screamed again.

I don't know if it was the piercing shriek or the kick to the face that did it (the shriek was my bet; it was devastating), but the thing let go. I pulled Sophie as she stomped on the ground. Her shriek apparently was not as devastating as mine. Whatever it was below the straw still had a hold on her.

I stomped around randomly until my ankle was once again enveloped. I kicked at it and pulled Sophie at the same time.

Sophie yelled again, so I pulled harder. I pulled my leg and Sophie free. We stumbled backward and fell into a heap of knees and elbows. I think they were all ours. For a split second, I thought we had passed through whatever it was that attacked us. But I was wrong. Dead wrong.

Huge figures began to rise from underneath the straw. By the time we got to our feet, there were at least six knights standing before us. They all wore armor. One was close enough to see his face. Or its face.

And then I remembered the bard's song: In the deep of the Dragon's Keep, the Knights of the Undead guard the dragon's egg. Ahh, farts.

I grabbed Sophie's hand and yelled, "Run!" It was quickly becoming our motto.

"Which way?" Sophie asked.

"The other way!" I said, pulling her toward the door I had seen earlier.

The knights followed behind, clanking as they walked like zombies across the room.

We reached the door. I shook the handle frantically until it opened. We thrust ourselves into the room, again falling to the ground.

"Lock it!" Sophie yelled.

We scrambled to our feet as a knight zombie approached the doorway. I grabbed the door and slammed it shut. Sophie fiddled with the lock until it clanked shut. We took a deep breath and leaned our backs up against the door, exhaling a relaxing breath.

The door boomed behind us as a clanky zombie arm pounded on the opposite side of the door.

"Would you think less of someone who tinkled in their tights? Just asking for a friend," I said.

"I was going to ask you the same question," Sophie said.

There was a tiny light illuminating a shiny yellow egg, a little smaller than a football, sitting atop a waist-high stand made of stone.

"Wow, this is so easy. There's no dragon. No fire. The egg's just sitting there," I said.

We walked over to it and studied it from every angle.

"No trip wires or anything," Sophie added.

The Knights of the Undead continued pounding on the doors. It echoed throughout the room.

"Let's just grab it and get the heck out of here."

"You do it," Sophie said.

"Just grab it," I said, faking frustration.

"You're supposed to be the hero."

"Says Lady Legend."

"Okay, I'm scared," Sophie said.

"Me, too."

The pounding on the door grew louder. We had to raise our voices to hear each other.

"We'll do it together," Sophie said. "On the count of three. One, two, three."

Sophie grabbed the egg. She stared me down. She looked like she was about to burn me with dragon's breath.

"What happened to going on the count of three?"

"I thought you were just demonstrating how you were gonna count. I didn't know it was the real one," I said.

"Ugh, seriously?"

"Sorry," I whispered. "The good news is that we didn't get scorched by a dragon, the walls didn't cave in, releasing a giant boulder that runs us down like in Indiana Jones."

"Let's get out of here. They're gonna break the door down."

We searched around every nook and cranny of the place. Yes, those are official medieval terms. It was sealed shut.

"There's no way out!" Sophie yelled.

Well, except for one way.

"We have to go out the way we came," I said, defeated.

"So easy," Sophie said, sarcastically.

"I think we should just live here. How many calories do you think this thing is?" I asked Sophie, holding the dragon's egg up and weighing it in my hands.

The knight zombies continued pounding on the door.

"They're coming," I whispered. I took a deep breath. "Okay, think, Austin," I said, with no thoughts whatsoever coming to me.

The pounding continued. "They're gonna blast right through the door any second!" Sophie yelled.

"What did you say?" I asked.

"They're gonna blast through the door!"

Blast! I looked at Sophie and said, "Okay, here's what we're gonna do. Remember what my dad said Mr. Muscalini would do?"

"Would do when? When he's facing knight zombies?"

"That's something new, but the same general idea. You know what I'm talking about! The 44 Blast! You're the running back. I'm the fullback. I'm going to clear a path!" I yelled.

"Or we could open the door and hide behind and hope they all walk past us," Sophie said. "We're not exactly football players and they're wearing armor."

"You're right. We're gonna die."

The pounding on the door was so severe, dirt fell from the ceiling above us and the wooden door began to splinter and crack.

"We have to hurry!" Sophie said, grabbing my arm.

"Let's combine the hiding and the 44 Blast. When they hit it hard, let's open it. Let them think they blasted it open and then we blast them," I whispered. "Ready?" I asked.

"No," Sophie whispered.

"Then let's go," I said, unlocking the door and pulling it open.

We jumped behind the swinging door, out of the way of the knight zombies. The knights clanked in, groaning like, well, really scary zombies. At least, I figured they sounded like zombies. It was my first zombie attack, so forgive me for not be able to compare it to others.

We held our breath and the door to our noses as we hid. I could hear knights continuing to clank past us, so we continued to wait, trying not to breath too heavily. I tried to peek out from behind the door to see what was going on, but I didn't want to stand out too far in case any of the knights saw me. I pulled the door tight to our noses. Sophie's hand joined me on the knob.

The clanking was getting farther and farther away. It was only a matter of time until they found us. We needed to move. Before I could tell Sophie it was time to go, the door handle ripped from my grip. The force pulled Sophie and I forward. I stumbled, but stayed on my feet while Sophie fell to her knees and forearms. I heard something bounce onto the ground.

Sophie yelled, "Oh, no!" and then scrambled across the floor on her knees.

The dragon's egg disappeared into the darkness. Sophie continued crawling on the floor and then turned with the dragon's egg under her arm. She looked up to see a knight zombie standing over her. The knight zombie pulled a sword from its sheath and raised it above its head.

I surged forward with every ounce of strength that I had and yelled, "44 Blast! Boo-ya!" I don't know why I threw the boo-ya in, but I felt it fit in the moment. You can judge, but if you've never been attacked by knight zombies, you should keep your pie hole shut.

I crashed into the knight zombie with epic force. It was nearly a head taller than me, twice as thick, and protected by armor, so to say that it hurt would be an understatement, but what I had going for me was the element of surprise. The knight stumbled back and then fell to the ground with an echoing clank.

"Dude! That hurt!" the knight zombie complained.

How do you think I felt, knight zombie? I mean, really. I figured regular zombies would have no consideration, but knight zombies should at least have some sense of valor and chivalry. I was pretty disappointed.

But I felt like I didn't have time to sulk. There were at least five more zombies clanking toward us. Sophie was on her feet. I grabbed her hand. We spun around toward the door. There was one Knight between us and the door.

"44 Blast!" I yelled.

Sophie added, "Boo-ya, punks!"

The 'punks' was a fabulous addition. That's just one of the many reasons I was totally crazy about her.

I ran toward the knight as fast as I could and added a little bit of gusto to it. I jumped and curled myself into a ball, knees first, and crashed into the knight zombie, like a cannon ball blast. We both fell to the ground on the other side of the door, the other knights clanking their way toward us.

Sophie hopped over the fallen knight and pulled me to my feet. We sprinted through the room and toward the stairs. Adrenaline was surging through my body. I ran up the stairs and thrust my arms up at the doors above my head. They blasted open with a crash. Sophie and I hopped out of the Dragon's Keep and slammed the doors for good measure. I wasn't sure if they would follow us, but I had no plans to find out.

I pulled Sophie as we ran back the way we came, toward the stables.

Sophie called to me, "The egg! I dropped it!"

"You what?" I shrieked. I slowed to a stop and turned to her.

"Just kidding," she said, holding the golden egg up into the afternoon sun. It was almost as beautiful as she was.

24

Trumpets blared across Chester. Sophie and I looked at each other. I could see the disappointment in her face and I could feel it throughout my whole body.

"Oh, no!" Sophie said.

"What's that for? Is it over? Did we lose?"

"I don't know. But everyone will be gathering at the great hall. Whoever has enough jewels can present themselves to the Protectors for judgement."

"We have more than jewels. We just have to get there quickly."

"But it's all the way on the other side of Chester. How are we going to get there in time?"

"What do we do best when on a quest?" I asked.

"Run!" Sophie said and took off.

I followed a few feet behind Sophie, running as fast as I could. She was putting some distance between us. After about a minute, I yelled out, "Wait!"

Sophie stopped at the tree line to wait for me. I caught

up, huffing and puffing. I leaned up against the tree. "This... isn't...gonna work," I said.

"You need to play fewer video games," she said.

"Agreed," I said, "but I can't do anything about that now."

Something caught my eye past the tree line. I stared out into the distance.

"What's the matter?" Sophie asked. "We have to hurry!" She looked in the same direction that I was looking in. And then her eyes saw the gloriousness that mine did. A stable of horses.

"Are you thinkin' what I'm thinkin'?" I asked.

"I'll beat you there!" Sophie said and took off running.

"Not exactly what I had in mind," I groaned as I followed.

As we approached the stable, I chuckled. There was a portapotty just next to the stable with piles and piles of chainmail, armor suits, and helmets.

"Looks like all the workers got fed up with the shortcomings of chainmail."

"What's the problem with it?" Sophie asked.

I pointed to the portapotty.

"Oh," she said, sheepishly.

We walked past the portapotty and peered around the corner where the entrance appeared to be. My spirits dropped. A man sat on a stool outside the main gate, guarding the stable. We ducked down around the corner to strategize.

"Should we break in from a window or another door and steal the horse? Should we pretend we're supposed to be there and take one?" I asked.

"Should we pretend first and break in second?" Sophie asked.

"What if the pretending goes wrong and then he goes into high alert?"

"What if we do both at the same time?" Sophie asked.

"Split up?"

"Yeah. Can you ride?" Sophie asked.

"A little. You?"

"Same."

"I could slap on some of that chainmail and attempt to get him to give me a horse. In the meantime, you could already be hiding inside, ready to borrow a horse if things go wrong."

"Okay," Sophie said, "but how do we get inside?"

"There have to be windows for the horses, right? I'll throw on some chainmail and you check around back, okay?"

"Yep," Sophie said and took off running around the back of the stable.

I headed back to the portapotty and piles of chainmail. I scoured all of the equipment for something that would come close to fitting. I found a helmet that was okay. It was a little loose, but manageable. The chainmail was a little more difficult. Apparently, chainmail doesn't have kids' sizes.

Sophie returned as I was sliding on a piece of chainmail. It was basically a mesh shirt of metal. Well, for me, it was less of a shirt and more of a dress. It didn't really match my shoes or my bag, but I had no time to go shopping.

"I was able to open one of the windows and the stall was empty. I can hop in there and hide. If you help me. Nice look, by the way. I like you shiny."

"Thanks, I may get one of these for school. If my lungs don't collapse from the weight of it."

She waved for me to follow her, which I did. We rushed around the back of the stable. She pried open the wooden window, which opened like shutters. The bottom of the now open window was about chest height.

"Here, let me give you a boost," I said, kneeling down on my hands and knees.

"So chivalrous," Sophie said as she stepped on my iron back and hopped over the wall with the stealth of a ninja.

I stood up as she faced me.

"There are a few options," she whispered. "I think if you can get him to at least open the main doors, I can make my way out."

"Okay," I said with a nod. "Good luck."

Sophie smiled. "And Godspeed, my prince."

I rushed around the side of the stable and then jogged up to the man with my helmet under my arm.

The man sat up in his chair, fresh from a nap. He looked at me, confused. I wasn't sure if it was me or that was his normal gaze.

"How about chainmail and portapotties? Not a good combo. I mean, am I right?" I slipped on my helmet, but kept the visor up.

"I guess so. Never wore the stuff." He looked down at his oversized belly, seemingly indicating to me the reason my chainmail wasn't part of his medieval wardrobe.

"Well, I guess tights aren't much better," I said, trying to build a connection.

"What are you doing here?" he asked me.

I used my best English accent, which was far from good, as I said, "I require my noble steed, but of course. I'm late for the coronation!"

"I didn't hear anything about that, dude."

I straightened up, flipped down my visor, and said, "It's Sir Dude to you, peasant boy. Now, fetch me my horse!"

"What did you say? I couldn't hear you with the visor."

I flipped the visor back up and said, "It's Sir Dude to you, peasant boy. Now, fetch me my horse!" I flipped the visor down with a clank.

The man looked me up and down and said, "I'm gonna have to call this one in." He picked up his belly, revealing a fanny pack. It was not a great sight. He unzipped the fanny pack and pulled out a walkie-talkie.

I couldn't risk him calling it in. I didn't know if Derek or Principal Butt Hair were listening to the air waves.

"There were no walkie talkies in medieval times!" I yelled. I grabbed the walkie talkie and chucked it with a grunt.

The walkie talkie helicoptered through the air. It smacked into a tree with a crack and fell into the brush below.

I looked the man up and down. He was big with a sagging, round belly. He was not exactly in Olympic running shape, but I was no track star, either. Plus, I was saddled with heavy chainmail. It was pretty evenly matched.

I grabbed the main door and slid it open as I started running. The man muttered under his breath and took off running after me. I ran out into the field, the man still chasing me. It was a big commitment on his part for one walkie talkie, which as we both know, had no right to be there. Neither did the fanny pack, for that matter.

He was roughly thirty feet behind me and slowing down. And then, bursting from the stable was a beautiful white horse, saddled with my future princess, Sophie. The horse galloped toward us, quickly gaining on the guard. He looked back with surprise as Sophie passed him with a smile.

"Hey! What are you doing?" he yelled.

I stopped as Sophie reached me in only a few seconds. She smiled, her curly hair wild from the ride.

Sophie shifted back in the saddle. "You coming?" She asked, while holding out a hand.

"I was thinking of a scenic walk," I said with a smile. I grabbed the reins with one hand and then hers with the other.

The guard walked toward us slowly, his hand on his hip, breathing heavy. "Don't go anywhere," he said between breaths. "I just wanna talk."

Yeah, right. The just-wanna-talk defense. I wasn't gonna fall for it. Apparently, the guard realized that and started running toward us again. My eyes bulged. I stepped into the stirrup as the horse looked back at me, and then it took off running.

I don't know if the horse caught its reflection in my armor and got scared at my fierceness or realized it was having such a bad hair day, but either way, it wanted to get the heck out of there.

"Ahhh, farts!" I yelled, as I tried to climb up onto the horse.

The bounce of the horse caught me off guard, tossing my foot out of the stirrup. I held onto the reins and grabbed the knob on the saddle while Sophie tried to pull me up, but it was no use. My hand slipped from the knob and I fell to the ground with a clank, my helmet vibrating so much I felt like my head was the gong that Mr. Muscalini whacked to start the quest. The horse dragged me for a bit, which made for the worst wedgie in the history of wedgies.

"Austin! Let go of the reins!" Sophie yelled.

I slipped my hand out of the reins that had been wrapped around my wrist, Sophie and the horse leaving me behind in a cloud of dust and dishonor.

Sophie yelled, "The guard is still coming. You gotta get up!"

I didn't want to get up. I wanted to lay there in my metal dress and tights for the rest of my life, but then I realized that my life was going to be really short once the guard caught up to me.

I rolled over onto my side as Sophie returned with our less than noble steed. The guard was only thirty feet away, which meant I had a solid five minutes before he got to me. I stood up, dusted myself off, checked SnapChat, and wrote a song for Sophie about riding horses together.

Sophie held the reins tight as I approached the horse. The horse turned its head toward me.

"Don't look at me," I said. "Look, a unicorn!"

The horse's head snapped back in the other direction. By the time it turned back around to stare me down for my trickery, both my feet were solidly in stirrups and my hands gripping the reins.

I slapped the reins down on the horse and yelled, "Hyaaaa!"

We took off as Sophie wrapped her arms around my waist. I hoped I didn't smell like worms and wedgie.

I looked back as the guard reached for the strap on the stirrup as we took off.

"Thanks for the help!" I called out with a wave.

We rode off down the path toward the great hall to lay claim to the throne.

25

S ophie and I galloped past the riddle station and then the jousting station. There were a bunch of adults and little kids, but nobody that we knew.

"I think the coronation is definitely happening," I yelled back to Sophie.

"Seems so. We'll stop it," she said, firmly.

We galloped through an open field. The archery station was up ahead. We were pretty close to the center of town and the great hall.

"We need some ammo!" Sophie yelled. "Stop at the archery station!"

"You want me to stop?"

After about a minute, we slowed as we entered the archery area.

The supervisor from the jousting station that tried to capture us after Randy accused us of cheating stood with his back to us as we approached. He was talking with another attendant.

Kids and adults both stared at us as we made our way through.

Sophie smiled at the father of some kid and said, "Sir, would you mind handing me a bow and a quiver full of arrows? I need it for the coronation ceremony."

The man smiled and said, "Sure." He stepped up to the equipment area and grabbed what we needed. He held it out to Sophie, but was distracted.

The supervisor from the jousting station yelled, "Stop! Criminals!"

The man froze. Sophie grabbed the bow and quiver from his hands.

"We already escaped from prison!" I yelled. My mother would be proud.

I slapped the reins down on the saddle and we took off.

"Thanks," Sophie called back to the man and then to me, "Hurry!"

Our horse picked up steam. We hit our stride just as we saw the outer circle of the town center. People were still strolling about despite the coronation that we assumed was taking place. I wasn't exactly an experienced rider through traffic. I had ridden a horse a few times in open spaces, but never with hordes of people around. And it showed. We steamrolled through the main part of town like a runaway train. We may have knocked over a few old ladies, but it wasn't on purpose. And in our defense, they were really slow and had bad eyesight. All the younger people saw us coming and dove out of the way with a few hundredths of a second to spare.

"Sorry" I yelled to an old lady who shook her cane at us menacingly as we passed.

Sophie yelled, "Ahh, farts!"

I looked ahead of us. 'Ahh, farts' was right. We approached the prisoner platform at full speed. I felt like I was going to puke, because the horse looked like it was going to run straight through the turkey leg vendor and across the platform that held the prisoners. I pulled back on the reins, but the horse didn't listen. And then he did. Like, a lot.

The horse stopped hard just before the turkey leg vendor, digging his front hooves into the ground, and kicked his hind legs into the air. I was a little upset that the horse wanted a food break when we were already late.

The force of the abrupt stop threw me from the horse's back. I soared through the air, Sophie still gripping me around the waist. I headed straight for Zorch, who remained locked in the stockades. I put down my visor as I approached impact. It was going to be ugly, but I was fully armored. I let out a manly shriek as I approached the stockade, turkey legs flying through the air.

My shoulder collided with the base of the stockade. I screamed in pain as I connected, the metal clanking loudly. My brain sizzled for a moment.

And then I heard Zorch say, "Oh, no." And then wood cracking.

Zorch groaned and teetered over on top of me.

Children were crying.

An old man, said, "Sir Frederick the Flatulent is dead."

As if our entrance wasn't bad enough, some dude yelled, "Free turkey legs!" And then the whole place erupted into chaos.

Zorch/Sir Frederick rolled off me and groaned, "Thanks, I guess."

A guard helped me to my feet. Zorch staggered to his. Thankfully, Sir Frederick the Flatulent wasn't dead. He would be flatulating for years to come.

I scanned the platform, looking for Sophie. Ben, Ditzy Dayna, Sammie, Just Charles, and Cheryl Van Snoogle-

Something sat in a line across the platform, their hands tied with one long rope, stretching across their laps. Figures.

Lord Dinkledorf yelled, "Sophie!"

I followed his gaze and flipped up my visor to see Sophie laying on the ground, her eyes closed. "My lady!" I yelled. I took off my helmet and threw it.

"Oww, my pinkie toe," Thaddeus whined.

"Sorry." I said as I dropped to my knees, hovering above Sophie.

"Only a knight's sweet kiss can wake her!" someone yelled.

"True love's kiss!"

Mr. Gifford whispered mysteriously, "It has been foretold."

The crowd chanted, "Kiss her! Kiss her!"

I didn't want to kiss her. Well, I wanted to kiss her, but I didn't know if she wanted to kiss me back.

"Fools! We need a doctor!" Lord Dinkledorf yelled.

"Aren't you a doctor?" Ditzy Dayna asked.

"Of philosophy! Not a medical doctor!"

"Yeah, but we call you doctor?"

I glanced quickly at Ditzy Dayna and then back at Sophie. I saw Sophie's eyes open and then close quickly. She puckered her lips slowly.

I exhaled. She was okay. I leaned in and kissed her. She opened her eyes as we stared at each other for a moment and then both smiled.

Sophie sat up and then I pulled her up with both hands and hugged her. The crowd cheered.

"Are you okay?" I asked.

"Yes," she said.

"You sure?" Zorch asked.

"Yes. I landed on a bunch of turkey legs."

"You signed the waiver, right?" Sir Thaddeus asked, concerned.

"Yes," Sophie said, rubbing her shoulder.

I looked around not sure of what to do. Sir Thaddeus, Lord Dinkledorf, and Sir Geoffrey the Gregarious/Mr. Gifford were still locked in the stockades and most of my friends were tied up, obviously having failed at their rescue mission.

The guard standing next to me stared blankly at me. I unsheathed his sword from his belt and held it underneath his chin. "Release the prisoners or I shall end you!" I said to cheers.

Sophie and Sir Frederick did the same to the guards near them.

The guard in front of me said, "I don't get paid enough for this." He took out his keys and unlocked the rest of the prisoners.

Sophie and Sir Geoffrey untied the rest of my crew.

"Be gone!" I yelled at the guards. "I banish you from Chester!" I wasn't sure if I had the authority to do that, but nobody stopped me.

Lord Dinkledorf thrust his fist in the air as we all yelled, "Huzzah!"

"You're late!" Lord Dinkledorf yelled. "Just go! You have to stop the coronation! We're right behind you!"

I adjusted the bag on my back as Sir Geoffrey handed me my helmet. "This is why you give me romantic advice." Mr. Gifford, the poor guy.

I put the helmet on and slammed down the visor. I walked over to the horse and grabbed onto the saddle.

"That's my horse, you know," Sir Thaddeus said.

"He rides like a dream. When he's not running down old ladies and tossing me like a salad," I said.

I kicked over the horse's back and settled my armored-self down.

Thaddeus helped Sophie onto the horse in the saddle behind me. He handed her the bow and quiver, and then smacked the horse's butt. The horse took off running again. Lucky us. The crowd cheered as we galloped toward the great hall.

As we approached the coronation, I could see that the

doors to the great hall were shut. I hoped that the coronation hadn't started yet. But the doors didn't stop us. I knew
better than to try to stop this horse. He ran right through the
doors, leaving an outline in them with his body and my
head. Just kidding. The horse stopped and kicked the doors
open with his front legs. It was pretty sweet Kung-Fu.

We burst through the doors as the stunned crowd
looked on. Even Emperor Buthaire's harpist stopped playing. Yeah, he was that much of an idiot. He had a harpist.
But no one was more stunned than Randy and Regan, who
knelt before the Emperor, apparently in the middle of
getting coronated, if that's a word.

I winked at Randy and then realized my visor was still
down. Ahh, farts.

26

I lifted my visor, winked at Randy, and then trotted into the middle of the great hall, all eyes on us. Randy and Regan spewed hatred. Emperor Buthaire was so shocked that he stared at us with his smile still half on his face and his goblet in the air, seemingly frozen.

Sophie let go of me as I pulled (very gently) on the reins. The horse slowed to a stop. Within a split second, I heard an arrow whizzing by my ears. I whipped my head around to follow the suction-tipped arrow as it cut through the medieval air, heading straight for Emperor Buthaire. His eyes bulged as it approached and connected with his goblet with a plop.

Pockets of the crowd cheered. "Huzzah!"

Emperor Buthaire plucked the arrow off his goblet, chuckled, and then tossed it to the floor. He pointed at us and yelled, "Seize them!"

The crowd booed.

Ben, Ditzy Dayna, Sammie, Just Charles, and Cheryl Van Snoogl-Something walked into the great hall and toward the stairs.

I looked at Ben as he mouthed, "Did I miss anything?"

I shook my head with a chuckle and then looked at Derek, standing in full armor behind Emperor Buthaire, and yelled, "Traitor!"

Sammie broke off from our crew, rushed past us, and said, "I must go to him. My prince!"

"Sammie, no!" I yelled.

"Where are the Protectors?" Sophie whispered.

"They're not here. We have to do something. We can't wait for them."

"We have to persuade them. Make our case to Buthaire."

"Would've been easier before you archered the Emperor."

"Archered isn't a word," Sophie said.

"I stand by it."

Guards made their way toward us, but appeared uneasy about the horse.

"I would like to say a few words!" I yelled.

Emperor Buthaire spat, "What say you, peasants?"

"You're gonna have to suck up a little," Sophie whispered.

"Yeah, I know. Archered," I said through gritted teeth. I looked at Emperor Buthaire and forced a smile. "Wise Emperor, 'tis an honor to serve you as a Knight of the Realm!" I nearly choked on my words, disgusted to my core.

I continued, "My lady and I wish to present ourselves for your consideration as Prince and Princess of the Realm!" I threw a "Huzzah!" in for good measure. A few people in the crowd echoed it.

Emperor Buthaire smiled and clapped. "Nice speech, Sir Suck Up, but you're too late."

"It's never too late for justice!"

The guard from the stable just arrived, probably via golf cart and yelled out, "He stole a horse! Justice for Buttercup!"

Buttercup? Really? I was thinking he was more of a "War Savage" or at least "Brego", Aragorn's great horse from Lord of the Rings.

"We borrowed the horse," I said. We had to get this back on track before the crowd turned on me.

"Emperor, surely you would make an exception for those that slayed the sleeping dragon?" I yelled to the crowd.

Chatter rose throughout the crowd.

"No way."

"That's impossible!"

"Did somebody fart?"

Emperor Buthaire yelled, "Zipeth your lipeth! Ye did nothing of the sorteth!"

I don't think any of those were words. I held my hand out. "My lady?"

Sophie reached into the bag on my back and said, "Uh, oh."

"My lady?" I asked, concerned.

"It split in two," she whispered.

"There's crazy glue in my bag."

"Really?"

"Of course not. Just hold it up together." I looked at the crowd. "Be right with you!"

"Just one second," Sophie mumbled.

"Is there a lot of dragon goop in my bag?" I whispered as Sophie fumbled inside the bag.

"No, the egg is foam."

"Oh, that's disappointing," I shrugged.

Sophie held up the dragon's egg with both hands.

Emperor Buthaire's eyes widened in surprise.

The crowd yelled, "Huzzah!"

27

The crowd returned to silence as it awaited the Emperor's decision. Emperor Buthaire stared at us. "How do we know it's the real egg?"

"You could've bought that dragon's egg at any 7-Eleven."

"There were no 7-Eleven's in medieval times!" someone yelled from the crowd.

"It's the real egg," I said, confidently.

"We are to believe that you, Sir Dinky Davenport, stole the dragon's egg from the Keep? The same task that Sir Thaddeus deemed impossible?"

The crowd's chatter began to rise. It did not appear to be supportive of Sophie and me. I took a deep breath and hopped off the horse. I looked up at Sophie and said, "I've got this."

"What are you going to do?"

"It ends where it began," I said, simply.

"Nice dress!" Randy called out to me. Regan, Emperor Buthaire, Derek, and some of the crowd laughed.

I ignored them and walked toward Randy. He stood up and faced me.

I swallowed hard and then yelled, "I challenge thee to a duel for the crown! I will crush ye like the turd that ye are."

Randy scoffed. "Again with the turds?" He exhaled and thought for a moment. "You're going to let me beat you up?" He had the same ecstatic look on his face that Derek did during our training.

I forced a laugh. "As if you can." I said it a lot more confidently than I felt.

Sophie whispered, "You don't have to do this."

I turned and used my best English accent, "But I must, my lady. For you desire the crown. And I desire your happiness. I will win you the crown. Or die trying!" I yelled, raising my fist in the air.

The crowd yelled, "Huzzah!"

Sophie frowned. "I think you're taking this a little too far."

"Maybe!"

Randy yelled out, "I will crush you in honor of my lady, the rightful princess and our esteemed emperor!"

The crowd voted its approval with raucous cheers.

I waited, holding my breath for the emperor's answer. After a brief moment, he bellowed, "I think we all desire a little entertainment and to see Austin's buffoonery."

"It's Sir Austin's buffoonery," I corrected him.

The crowd went crazy. Everybody was itching for a fight. I had revenge in mind. There were so many things I owed Randy payback for, I couldn't even count them.

I stood in front of Sophie, clutching my sword, with Ben at my side. The crowd's loyalty was split. There were loud cheers of both, "Sir, Aus the Boss," and "Oh, my God, did you see him shake out his hair! It moves in slow motion!"

While we waited for Randy to get geared up, Sophie

looked into my eyes and said, "Good luck. No matter what happens, you're already my prince."

"That's beautiful," Ben said, whimpering.

I smiled. "I know. I feel the same way about you."

"I'm your prince?" Sophie asked.

"You know what I mean. Now, excuse me while I win us our kingdom."

As I was walking out to meet Randy in the center of the great hall, Ben hustled over to me. "I almost forgot to tell you. I saw Max. He told me to remind you of The Thing. He said you would know what he was talking about. I have to tell you that I'm a little disappointed that you talk Fantastic Four with people besides me."

"It's not like that, Ben," I said. Energy surged through my veins.

Ben looked me in the eye and jumped back, startled. "Whoa! What's gotten into you?"

"I'm ready for battle!"

"I have one word of my own for you," Ben said and then paused for effect. "Bubbles."

"Bubbles!" I yelled, thrusting my sword in the air. Everybody looked at me like I was a wacko.

I turned and stared at Randy. He would expect me to be timid and on the run, so I charged at him at full force. With the chainmail, it probably looked like slow motion. I hoped it was still cool, even though it wasn't Randy's hair. I screamed, "I'm gonna pop you like a bubble!"

Our swords clashed above our heads, Randy barely blocking my savage attack. I followed with a kick to the stomach. It wasn't hard, but enough to stun him and push him back. I followed with a horizontal strike to his shoulder. My sword clanked with his chainmail, sparks flying from the force of it. Team Sir Aus the Boss cheered wildly. Randy's visor was down, but I was certain he was no longer smirking. Unless it was permanent? It was definitely possible.

Randy circled around quickly, his long legs an advantage over my stubby ones. I followed, readying for another attack, but his hands were quick. He swung his sword like a baseball bat and connected with my iron abs, the force of which caused me to spit, which was nicely captured by the inside of my helmet. Better spit than blood, I always say.

I methodically sliced and stabbed every bubble I saw on Randy. He blocked some, absorbed others. He didn't have the sword skills that I had developed, but he was bigger, stronger, and faster. I did my best to block and counter his attacks whenever I could, but some were just too fast and too hard to stop.

"Circles and angles!" Ben yelled.

I yelled a muffled, "Thank you!" and then sidestepped Randy's next attack, which came slicing down from above his head.

I jabbed him with the butt of my sword on the shoulder, as my hands were too close to do anything else while I slipped my foot behind his. Randy crashed to the ground, his back landing first and then his head.

The crowd was stunned to silence. I was so shocked I just stood over Randy, my lungs begging for air, staring at him. It was not the smartest thing I could've done.

"Finish him!" someone from the crowd bellowed.

Before I could do anything, Randy swung his sword from the ground in an arc, connecting with the backs of my knees. I fell forward with a groan. My legs had no armor. The force pushed me forward as the sword slipped from my hands and I landed on my chest.

I scampered up and grabbed my sword as Randy also got to his feet. He chased me as I gripped my sword. I blocked his stabbing attack and countered with an overhand attack of my own, which knocked him backward, but he parried to the side. My sword tip continued to the ground and stuck.

Randy steadied himself with the sword in his left hand and a fist in his right. I remembered what my brother had said, "Randy can't go left." I reached for my sword, but it was too late. A fist full of dirt and small pebbles cut through the air, heading straight for my helmet. I turned my head, but a second too late. Dirt pelted my eyes through the small slit in the visor.

The crowd booed as I staggered around, feeling for my sword.

"To your left!" Sophie yelled.

I lifted my visor and wiped my eyes. I turned around in a circle, trying to get my bearings.

"Your other left!" Ben yelled.

I looked to my left. My sword stood calmly stuck in the ground. Randy, on the other hand, was surging toward me, sword above his head as he screamed, "Peasantfart!"

My training kicked in. I dove to the side and rolled out of the way of Randy's attack. The crowd cheered.

I got to my knees and tugged on my sword as Randy's sliced through the air headed straight for my side. I lifted the sword and parried the blow, but it knocked the sword out of my hand. It skidded across the ground as I stumbled back and crashed into the railing. I leaned against it, still not fully able to see.

The crowd booed. Ben yelled, "Cheater!"

Even though I was unarmed, Randy came at me again. I dodged his overhead attack. His sword smashed the wooden railing into splinters. I ran for my sword, but still off balance, I fell to the ground. I rolled over as Randy walked up beside me, twirling his sword in his hand.

He stood over me with his signature smirk. There was nothing I could do. My sword was too far away. It was over. He held his sword above my chest with one hand and shook off his glove, revealing a gaudy, emerald ring.

"Kiss the ring, peasant! Swear your loyalty before this court and ye shall live!" It was a tad dramatic.

The crowd booed yet again.

Somebody yelled, "Never! He will die with honor!"

I wasn't certain that was the path I wanted to take, so I leaned forward and puckered my lips. I glanced up at

Randy. He was laughing while looking at the crowd. It was a perfect decoy.

I knocked his sword away with my hand and yelled, "Never! Austin Davenport will not be ruled!"

Team Sir Aus the Boss exploded into cheers.

I scrambled to my feet as Randy readied himself for battle yet again. I rushed to my sword and forced it above my head just in time to block another of Randy's vicious blows.

My arms shook as I pressed my sword against his. Randy grunted as he pushed his sword's blade closer and closer to my neck. And then he let up on the pressure, causing my hands to surge outward. Randy redirected his sword, encircling mine and smacking down on my hands. The sword slipped from my grip and arced across the great hall like a Hail Mary football pass. The crowd watched it as it flew toward the emperor and then split the wood at his feet. The sword swayed back and forth, stuck in the floor board of the platform.

The crowd fell silent. I fell to my knees, drained. My sword was out of reach. My body ached with exhaustion. I was so thirsty I would've considered buying a whole jug of dirty water, no matter the consequences.

Randy removed the helmet from his head and tossed it aside. He shook out his hair in slow motion. Some girls cheered.

No one knew what Randy would do as he spun the sword in his hand.

Regan yelled, "Doeth it!"

Randy looked down at me with a ruthless smile and squeezed the grip on his sword.

28

R andy hesitated for a moment, perhaps creating tension for the crowd, holding the final blow of his sword above his head. I gulped, too tired to do anything else. Out of the corner of my eye, I saw Regan inching closer, a look of evil glee across her face. If she had a sinister mustache, she would be twisting it.

Without warning, Randy's head snapped back with a fwop. With his sword back behind his head and the clunky armor, the force of whatever it was that hit him toppled him over. Randy fell back into a heap, his armor smacking the ground and reverberating. A suction-cupped tipped arrow stood straight up from his forehead.

I looked to my left to see Regan flat on her back as well, an arrow suctioned to her forehead.

The crowd stood in stunned silence. I turned my head to see Sophie still holding the follow through of her bow shot, a satisfied grin on her face.

After a few seconds of silence, the crowd exploded into a chaos of cheers and chants. They were a lot of "Huzzahs!" I can tell you that much.

Ben rushed over to me to help me up. "That was incredible!"

I stood up with a grunt. Sophie dropped her bow and ran to me. She jumped into my arms. I could barely keep from falling over.

"That was amazing!" Sophie yelled.

"I lost," I mumbled.

"No, we won! And he cheated...again."

I cracked a small smile that got wider as I thought about the battle. I did bash him pretty good a few times.

I looked over at Randy and smirked at the red mark still prominent on his forehead. Oh, man, did he deserve that.

"It looks like Sandy Wandy Randy just got his butt kicked," Just Charles said through laughter.

Randy glared at him.

Just Charles' face morphed serious as he added a "Sir."

Ditzy Dayna turned to Regan and mocked her, "Are you okay, Schmoopie?"

It was the first thing she said all day that made any sense.

Emperor Butt Hair stood up and clapped slowly. The rest of the crowd's excitement drained.

The emperor interrupted our moment as he spoke, "Excellent performance! 'Tis but one problem. In no realm shall I ever allow Austin Davenport to win, let alone be my heir. Sir Derek, Seize him!"

I froze as Derek took a step forward in obedience to his evil master, but before he could make it to the stairs, Sammie grabbed the emperor's goblet from the table and threw it as hard as she could. It toppled base over rim as it headed toward the back of Derek's armored head. It connected with a clank.

Derek turned to see what had hit him, but all I saw were the whites of his eyes as he crumpled to the floor in a heap of evil and metal.

"Huzzah!"

Emperor Buthaire yelled to the guards, "Seize him!"

The guards didn't move, except to look at each other.

"Do not disobey your emperor!" Emperor Butt Hair screamed, his face even more red than Mr. Muscalini's, and he was wearing makeup. "I order you to seize him, immediately!"

The guards drew their swords. The tension in the air was medievally heavy. The crowd whispered, not sure what was going to happen next.

Sophie and I looked at each other. She drew another arrow while I readied my sword.

"We don't run this time!" she yelled.

"Not today!" I answered, wanting to keep the option open to future running away.

The guards threw their swords down to the ground.

Emperor Buthaire looked around, eyes wide in panic. He pointed at Lady Dionisia the Deadly and Mazelina the Meh, and said, "It is time you prove your worth! Protect your emperor!"

Mazelina the Meh thought for a moment and then said, "Maybe later."

Lady Dionisia stood up and pounded the table with both fists. She had fire in her eyes as she drew her sword.

ady Dionisia walked toward Emperor Butt Hair, en route to the steps down from the platform, her eyes locked on mine. She was nearly as big as Mr. Muscalini with her chainmail on.

"I'll help, Emperor," Mr. Muscalini said as he walked over to Derek, who was sitting on his butt and rubbing the back of his head. Mr. Muscalini grabbed Derek's sword.

The trumpeters stepped forward. "So will we."

Emperor Buthaire smiled at me with satisfaction.

The trumpeters surrounded the emperor, held up their trumpets, and blasted them. The emperor grabbed his ears and fell to his knees. The harpist tried to play really loud, offensive music, but everyone just sighed. Some people even teared up.

Mr. Muscalini and Lady Dionisia pointed their swords at the defenseless emperor, whose eyes still appeared to be rolling around in circles.

The crowd cheered. Ben and Sophie hugged me.

"Look!" Luke yelled.

We all looked toward the entrance to the great hall. Lord

Dinkledorf, Sir Thaddeus, Sir Frederick the Flatulent, and Sir Geoffrey the Gregarious rode in on horses, followed by at least a dozen armed guards.

Sir Thaddeus drew his sword and said, "Simon the Serious, you have committed high treason! You shall be stripped of your knightly title and banished from The Realm forever!"

The crowd went crazy. People were hugging. Women and Mr. Muscalini were crying.

All Sir Thaddeus had to say was, "Guards!" and six guards rushed to the former emperor, lifted him to his feet, and escorted him out of the great hall.

Principal Buthaire looked at me and yelled, "This isn't finished. You will rue the day!"

Ben yelled, "Be thee gone!"

"Oh, knock it off, Butt Hair," Lord Dinkledorf said.

Mr. Gifford and Zorch both looked at him and said, "Mason, he's still our boss."

Lord Dinkledorf shrugged, turned to the crowd, and yelled, "Huzzah!"

The Protectors huddled for a moment and then Sir Thaddeus returned to the center of the great hall to address the crowd.

"It is time for the coronation!" Sir Thaddeus yelled, his sword in the air.

"Huzzah!"

"But who is to be the prince? The princess?"

Sir Thaddeus bellowed, "But of course, it shall be Sir Austin and Lady Sophie!"

Randy ran up to Sir Thaddeus and yelled, "You can't do that! Nobody said Sophie could do that. I beat him in a sword fight. Those arrows aren't even real!"

"From what I hear, you're lucky that they're not."

"Sorry, dude. I think you're kinda dead," Ben yelled.

"How is one kinda dead?" Randy asked.

Thaddeus stepped forward and whispered, "He's right, dude. You're dead." He pointed to Regan. "You, too. Now get down on the ground and play dead."

"I will not!" Regan yelled to laughter. "We're done, Randy! How could you humiliate me like this!" Regan stormed out.

Randy chased after her. "Regan, wait!" He followed her out of the great hall, disappearing into the night.

Sir Thaddeus turned back to the crowd and yelled, "Rejoice! The Realm is safe once again! I give you Prince Austin and Princess Sophie!" He pointed to us with a huge grin on his face.

The crowd celebrated with too many high fives and huzzahs to count. I grabbed Sophie's hand as we walked toward Sir Thaddeus. The crowd tossed flowers at us. I actually caught one and handed it to Sophie.

"We did it, my princess."

"You're my hero," she said with a smile.

"And you're my Lady Legend," I said.

"That's a bit much. If I let you call me that, I'd feel like Randy or something."

Sir Thaddeus said, "Do you have the egg?"

"Umm, it's broken," Sophie said.

"What about your crowns?"

"Busted," I said.

"Okay," Sir Thaddeus said, shrugging. "Then join me in revelry. We have a feast fit for a king! Chicken fingers!"

The crowd fell silent. Even Lady Mazelina was disappointed. She whispered, "That's it?"

Sir Thaddeus yelled, "I jest. Tonight, we feast on turkey legs!"

"Huzzah!"

COMING SOON!

NEW RELEASE ON 1/15/2020

NEW RELEASE ON 2/14/2020
(VALENTINE'S DAY- DUH...)

30

BOOK SIX PREVIEW CHAPTER

E verybody loves an underdog. Well, except for the overdogs. Is that even a word? If not, it should be. At Cherry Avenue Middle School, home of the ferocious Gophers, I was that beloved underdog. And I had three overdogs who loved stealing my bone and pooping on my front lawn. I mean, not literally. Well, one of them was my butt-chinned brother, Derek, and he set off a lot of bags of flaming poo on our front lawn, but they weren't always directed at me. Sometimes, they were in protest of something my parents had done. It was a strange way to protest, but my brother isn't exactly known for his sophistication. But he gets away with more than me because he has the family butt chin and I don't. Nobody said life was fair, kids.

Anyway, it was the first day back at school after the Medieval Renaissance fair, a fabulous place where I had made a handful of overdogs incredibly unhappy. I walked off the bus and into school half expecting the war with Principal Butt Hair (a term of endearment for our less-than likable Principal Buthaire), no, fully expecting, the war to continue. I wasn't expecting a Kung-Fu kick to the face right on the spot, but I hid in the shadows like a ninja just in case. I ducked behind the hulking Nick DeRozan, did a dive roll behind a bench, nearly concussed myself, and popped up behind one of the dogwood trees in the Atrium. Not only is it a weird name for a tree, but they were pretty thin and not overly helpful in providing ninja shade.

Thankfully, I made it to my Advisory class undetected. My buddy, Just Charles sat next to me. I know it's a strange nickname, but he kind of gave it to himself. People called him Charlie or Chuck so many times and he hated it. He would yell, "My name is just Charles!" It kinda stuck.

It didn't take long for Butt Hair to take his first shot at me. The Speaker of Doom crackled in the corner of the classroom. Just Charles looked at me. I smiled and stood up.

"That's my cue," I said.

Mrs. Callahan was busy writing something down. She didn't look up. "Please sit...oh, Austin, Mrs. Murphy already told me that you were getting called down."

And right on cue, Mrs. Murphy whined, "Austin Davenport to the principal's office for the thousandth time. And Sophie Rodriguez."

Say what? Sophie was my girlfriend. She never got in trouble, although she was my partner in the Medieval Renaissance quest, and she beat Emperor Buthaire just as badly as I did, if not more.

I walked as quickly as I could. I wanted to beat Sophie there. She would need my support. I figured she was in shell shock. I sat in the main office, waiting for her to show up so we could receive our first couple's detention from Prince Butt Hair. I'm a real romantic. The office was bustling with activity even more than usual. I didn't chart traffic patterns or anything, but when you're there as much as I was, you get a good feel for things. I furrowed my brow as I looked into the small office next to The Butt Crack, Principal Buthaire's office, to see a woman I didn't recognize. She was unpacking boxes.

The door squeaked open and Sophie walked in. Even though we were in the principal's office and yelling was likely to ensue shortly, I was still happy to see her. She forced a smile and slumped down into the seat next to me.

"Hey," I said.

Sophie took a deep breath. "Is this how it feels every time?"

"The sense of dread and extreme unfairness? Yep. And enjoy this one, because each one gets worse."

"Ugh," she said, putting her face in her hands.

"Is this your first time in the principal's office, ever?" I asked, somewhat amused.

"Yes. My parents are gonna be so happy. How many is this for you?"

"Lost count. I should be writing it all down so I could tell the planet's youth all about it, though. I think my story would be a global phenomenon."

"Yeah, I think you're right." Sophie looked into the office next to Principal Buthaire's and asked, "Who is that?"

"Probably a new office manager or something. Prince Butt Hair fires them like he changes his underwear."

"Never?"

I laughed and then turned it into a cough as Principal Buthaire emerged from The Butt Crack. His eyes bored into me. He didn't even say anything. He just pointed at me with two fingers and then down at the floor in front of him. Sophie and I stood up and walked over to his office. Even though I had been through it a hundred times, my pulse still pounded throughout my body.

Principal Buthaire lowered himself slowly into the chair

and then straightened his stapler and tie. He stared at us for a minute before speaking. "Do you know why you're here?"

"Because you ordered us to be?" I asked.

Principal Butt Hair shook his head slowly. "You are like an annoying little fly, Misterrrr Davenport. Buzzing, buzzing, buzzing in your ear. You try to swat it, but miss. You roll up a magazine or grab a fly swatter and take a few more swings. It's annoying when you keep missing, because they're pesky little creatures and they can make you look like a fool, but it's oh so satisfying when you finally connect and squash that annoying little fly. I take particular pleasure in watching it twitch before it takes its last breath."

I looked at Sophie. She was normally Wonder Woman under pressure, but her face was pale. She probably never understood the extent of how much of an idiot Principal Buthaire was. I've been known to exaggerate a thing or two, so maybe my friends didn't fully believe me when I told them all of my stories.

My eyes returned to Prince Butt Hair. "That's dark, sir."

"It's the circle of life. That's how the food chain works."

I wasn't a fly expert by any means, but I am a science genius, so I was pretty certain he was wrong, but I had learned over time that certain battles weren't worth fighting. I had enough big Butt Hair battles to deal with.

"Ms. Rodriguez, I hope this does not become a habit with you. I fear that if you continue to keep the same company, it will be." He stared at me as his voice shook with anger, "Bad influences will drag you down." Principal Buthaire looked back at Sophie. "I was particularly hurt by the arrow you shot at me during the Renaissance Fair. And for that, you get detention."

"That's not fair," I said. "It wasn't a school event."

Sophie said, "And it was rubber and it only hit your goblet."

"That's all well and good, but now you both get detention for arguing with your principal."

"That's not fair," Sophie said, stupefied.

"We were arguing because you were wrong," I said.

"THE DETENTION STANDS." Principal Buthaire reached into the inner pocket of his suit jacket and pulled out his best (and only) friend, his detention pad. He tore off two slips and handed them to us. "I'm in a good mood today. Hurry to class before you're late."

I stood up ready to sprint out of there before he changed his mind, but Sophie appeared frozen in her seat.

"Soph, time to go. Like, now," I said.

Sophie shook her head and stood up. I gently prodded her out of the office. I shut the door behind me, as we left to make sure he couldn't shout more detentions out at us from his chair.

The woman from the office next door stared at us as I ushered Sophie out of the office.

"It really gets worse than this?" Sophie asked.

"Pretty much every time. That was actually a good one, though. Definitely savor it. I wonder why the heck he was in a good mood after the Renaissance Fair?" What was I missing? I didn't even know it was possible for him to be in a good mood.

As I was getting my binder for English class, Just Charles and Cheryl Van Snoogle-Something walked by within a larger crowd of kids, all seemingly going in the same direction. They had been partners at the Medieval Renaissance fair quest that we all participated in. I wondered if there was a budding romance at hand. Just Charles was just like me, unsure why a girl like Cheryl was actually interested in him. I was the Cherry Avenue Gopher poster boy for having a girlfriend 'out of my league' with Sophie.

"What are you doing?" Just Charles asked, stopping beside me.

"Getting my books for class. What are you doing? Where is everyone going?"

"There's no class," Cheryl said. "There's an assembly."

Just Charles said, "Oh, yeah. You missed the morning announcements. Again. What did Butt Hair want?"

"To harass me. I love assemblies."

Sammie walked up and stopped to join the group. She was one of my besties, having grown up next door to me.

"Any idea what it is?" Cheryl asked.

"Beats me," Just Charles said. "The Speaker of Doom didn't say."

Sammie said cheerily, "I hope it's something cool."

"Like what?" Cheryl asked.

"I don't know. Maybe an author."

"Like who?"

"C.T. Walsh. That guy is awesome," Sammie said.

"Agreed. And so handsome," Cheryl said.

"Meh," Sammie said, shrugging.

Guys don't like talking about how handsome other guys are, no matter how cool C.T. Walsh was, and it was an off-the-charts level of cool. I hoped to meet him at Comic-Con during the summer. My dad said he would take us. But I had to change the subject. "Anybody seen Randy yet?"

"Thankfully, no," Just Charles said.

"I haven't, either," Sammie said, but she didn't appear to be as thankful as Charles. She had a crush on Randy last year and I wasn't sure if she was completely over it. Even though her taste in authors was superb, her taste in boys was the exact opposite.

"Slow down," I said, "so we don't have to see him. He's up front. Can't you see his big head up there?"

I looked across the Atrium. Through the crowd of assembly-goers, I could see two men installing some sort of video screen or scoreboard.

"What the heck is that?" I asked.

"Maybe it's so we can play video games between classes," Just Charles said, laughing.

"Yeah, right. It's more likely that Butt Hair streams videos of me getting yelled at. Sophie joined me in that fun endeavor this morning."

"I heard," Just Charles said. He turned to Sophie. "Sorry to hear."

Sophie just shrugged. "I just feel bad that Austin has to deal with that every week. He's such a jerk and so unfair."

"Who, Butt Hair?" Sammie asked, chuckling. "Not him." She rolled her eyes.

As we filed into the auditorium, I searched for signs of what was planned. I didn't see any handsome or not-so-handsome authors. No police officers or zoo animals. The assembly was a giant mystery.

Sophie and Ben joined our group as we grabbed seats in the middle of the auditorium. Most of our crew were nerds, but even we knew that it wasn't cool to sit too close up front. I sat down next to Sophie and settled in. Out of the corner of my eye, I saw Randy climbing over people in the row ahead of us. He stopped a few seats from us. He looked down at the dude in front of him and said, "You're in my seat."

The kid stood up quickly and scooted out of the row. Randy sat down. I hadn't realized it at first, but Regan was in the seat next to him. I wondered what was going on with the two of them after things ended, well, badly for them at the Renaissance Fair.

"Hey," he said to Regan with his fake smile.

She ignored him.

"You still mad at me?"

"You're good," Regan spat.

Randy smiled and said, "Thanks!" And then realized it wasn't actually a compliment. "How many times can I say it? I'm sorry."

"Don't care." Regan said icily and turned her body away from him.

Randy stared at me and said, "What're you looking at, Davenfart?"

"A train wreck," I said. I couldn't help myself, so I added, "Now you know how it feels to be treated like garbage."

"Shut your face, Davenfart," Randy said, his face red. He turned away with a huff.

Thankfully, the lights flickered and Principal Buthaire walked out onto the stage, a microphone in his hand. He was strutting his stuff like a dumb peacock. The place was dead silent, but based on the look on his face, you would think that he was getting a standing ovation. It was concerning. It was never a good sign when Butt Hair was happy. It meant he was going to make the rest of us unhappy.

"Good morning, Gophers!"

The crowd responded with a few grunts. Gary Larkin threw out a fake fart. Or maybe it was real. He was that good.

Prince Butt Hair continued, "I have been working on a secret project that has finally come to fruition."

Just Charles leaned toward me and asked, "What is he planting apple trees?"

"I just completed a global search for my protege and I am pleased, no, overjoyed, to introduce you to her."

A woman walked out to the stage, smiling. She was well dressed and proper. It was the same woman from the main office earlier.

Sophie whispered to me, "She looks nice. Maybe she won't be so bad."

"You think Butt Hair's protege is going to be nice? Who do you know that Butt Hair likes that is actually nice?"

"We can hope."

"Hope is a dangerous strategy when it comes to Cherry Avenue Middle School. I think our motto is actually, 'we crush children's hopes and dreams.'"

Sophie elbowed me with a smile.

Principal Buthaire continued his introduction. "Ms. Anne Pierre comes from the prestigious Academy of Worcester, a school with students much better than this one. We're lucky to have her. Let me read you her bio. It's quite impressive." He pulled out a piece of paper from his suit jacket as Ms. Pierre stood beside him, smiling at the crowd. "Ah, here we are." Principal Buthaire looked at Ms. Pierre and smiled. He read, "Ms. Pierre completed her teacher training at the Harvard Graduate School of Education. She is currently writing her PhD dissertation on Classroom Management and Student Behavior. She has a blessed balance of a nurturing spirit with firm discipline. She enjoys evening strolls with her dog, Monty, and moulding the minds of today's youth and tomorrow's leaders."

"Who is she, the Mary Poppins of Vice Principals?" Sophie asked.

Principal Buthaire put the paper away and said, "She is, without a doubt, going to shape our pedagogy for years to come here at Cherry Avenue Middle School."

"Pedawhoey?" Just Charles whispered.

"I thought he said something about petting a goat. I'm lost," I said with a shrug.

"Please give her a warm Gopher greeting. She's our new Vice Principal, Ms. Anne Pierre!"

There were more claps and cheers than I thought there would be, but I guess there was some hope that she would be an improvement over Principal Buthaire. She did sound like the Mary Poppins of Principaling.

"I don't want to overwhelm Ms. Pierre on her first day. I'll just ask her to give us a few words to describe what she wants to see during her time here."

"Pain," she said, pounding her fist into her palm, laughing maniacally. "Just kidding. I want to see the wonderful smiles of all these sweet children, as their brains expand and their friendships flourish."

ABOUT THE AUTHOR

C.T. Walsh is the author of the Middle School Mayhem Series, set to be a total twelve hilarious adventures of Austin Davenport and his friends.

Besides writing fun, snarky humor and the occasionally-frequent fart joke, C.T. loves spending time with his family, coaching his kids' various sports, and successfully turning seemingly unsandwichable things into spectacular sandwiches, while also claiming that he never eats carbs. He assures you, it's not easy to do. C.T. knows what you're thinking: this guy sounds complex, a little bit mysterious, and maybe even dashingly handsome, if you haven't been to the optometrist in a while. And you might be right.

C.T. finds it weird to write about himself in the third person, so he is going to stop doing that now.

You can learn more about C.T. (oops) at ctwalsh.fun

facebook.com/ctwalshauthor

goodreads.com/ctwalsh

instagram.com/ctwalshauthor

ALSO BY C.T. WALSH

Down with the Dance: Book One

Santukkah!: Book Two

The Science (Un)Fair: Book Three

Battle of the Bands: Book Four